Kieran's Light

A Midlife Beach Town Halloween Romance

Sadira Stone

To Duncan, my HEA

A Note to Readers:

This story contains brief portrayals of PTSD flashbacks and dreams.

I do not use generative artificial intelligence in any part of my writing process. All my books were written by me, with feedback from my human editor and human beta readers. Different "authors" may make different choices, but I believe the best art comes from human minds, spirits, and hearts. Take that, robot overlords!

Contents

Chapter One

♥

"It's a profound cosmic injustice." Scowling at the magnificent view—towering pines and cedars interspersed with maples and alders blazing scarlet and gold—Doctor Addyson Connor eased her BMW around yet another hairpin turn. Through a break in the trees, the Pacific shone jewel-blue, gilded by the late-afternoon sun.

Okay, so it was beautiful out here. But damn it to Kandahar and back, she'd wanted to share this weeklong leave on the Washington coast with her best friend. What's the point of a solo vacation?

"Sorry, Addy," Liv crooned in her soothing therapist voice, "You'll just have to make do with Snoot. He's a good listener."

Upon hearing his name through the car speakers, the chocolate Lab whined and wriggled as far forward as his seat harness allowed.

Addy reached over her shoulder and skritched him behind his floppy ears.

"Seriously, though," she grumbled, "if talking it out with doggo-face was the answer, I could've stayed home."

Liv's low chuckle filled the X-1's interior. "Everyone needs a break, sweetie, even gorgeous surgeons who exhaust themselves with work instead of dealing with their issues." Liv crunched into her phone—probably greasy egg rolls from the

AAFES food court in the military hospital where they both worked.

"Gorgeous? Hmmph." Addy glanced at her reflection: face ghostly pale from too much time indoors, dark hair wind-snarled into spaghetti, thanks to the window she left open on the three-hour drive from Joint Base Lewis-Mc-Chord. "Is it my fault the surgical schedule is so tight?"

"Gonna call bullshit on that one, sis. I have it on good authority you've been volunteering for extra procedures."

"Yeah, well..." Addy cranked the wheel hard as the road skirted a rocky outcropping. "It's either work or think about, you know, not-work."

"Why not talk this over with Enzo?"

"Ugh." Colonel Enzo Nardoni, her assigned therapist, talked too much and listened too little. "I know he's qualified and all—"

"When it comes to combat-induced PTSD, he's one of the best, Addy."

"Agree to disagree." Honestly, she'd rather rely on her own coping strategies than endure another pointless session with that bloviating bore. His bushy nose hair and condescending tone made her skin crawl.

Besides, her problems didn't stem from warfare itself, just the horrific aftermath. The things she'd seen in that combat support hospital—mangled limbs, shredded bellies, bone salad, inhuman screams, the coppery smell of blood...

Though Addy's body was unmarked by shrapnel wounds, her soul was crisscrossed with scars.

And she'd been counting on this relaxing week with Liv, AKA Lieutenant Colonel Olivia Williams, US Army psychologist. Even though their friendship precluded Liv from treating Addy, her thoughtful "um hmms" and sympathetic head nods had a magical way of lending clarity to the convoluted mess that was Addy's life.

Between pressure from her family in Nebraska, her punishing work schedule, and intrusive thoughts, it was harder and harder to keep the threads from unraveling. Her co-workers were starting to notice, too. Yesterday, Lieutenant Marco Ochinang, her favorite surgical nurse, stopped her on her way to the hospital's coffee shop for her third cup that afternoon and asked, "Ma'am, are you okay?"

She'd brushed off his concern with a forced smile, but judging by his skeptical expression, she was a shitty actor.

This vacation was supposed to be her chance to sort it all out: what to do about her ailing, venomous mother and the whole spiteful clan, plus the minor matter of where the hell to steer her career for the next twenty or so years. Liv had volunteered to help her talk through it—until an emergency on base had cancelled Liv's leave.

"How are they doing over at the Stryker Brigade?"

"Not great. Losing two young NCOs like that—" Liv gave a weary sigh. "And one of them was a new dad. As much as I hate it, Colonel Okafor made the right call. I'm booked solid for the next four days."

"Yeah, it's a heartbreaker." Addy had been called in for an emergency surgery on one of the backseat passengers, a military wife whose leg was so badly mangled by the crash, she'd probably limp for the rest of her life. Poor woman, just twenty-four and already a widow.

Then again, the widows she'd met downrange had been younger. Their grief-stricken wails haunted her dreams.

"Anyway," Liv said, "you're going to have a wonderful time. You've got your assignment, and I expect a full report."

"Right, right." Addy threw a glance over her shoulder. "I'll fill up that journal if Snoot doesn't eat it first."

"Snoot!" Liv snapped through the dashboard speaker. "No eating Mama's stuff."

The dog huffed and dropped the duffle bag handle he'd been chomping on.

"Good boy."

Addy's brow furrowed. "Did you hide a spy camera in my car?"

"Oh dear, what did he mangle this time?"

"No damage, just a little drool."

Liv's belly-shaking laughter rang out. "Now, I want you to promise me you'll give yourself the break you need, lovey. Walk the beach. Bring me back some shells—and something from Souvenir Planet."

"Another UFO mug?" Addy rounded the windy road's last curve, and the town of Trappers Cove came into view, its colorful shops stretched out along Main Street like a string of mismatched beads.

"Surprise me. Ope, there goes my pager. We'll talk soon. And hey, get yourself a yummy man while you're there. You've been sublimating your libido for far too long."

Liv signed off with a loud smooch, and Addy's road-trip playlist picked up in the middle of a song she and her friend should have been singing together. She grumbled, muted the nineties boy band, and cruised down Main Street, past restaurants, bars, and souvenir shops. Now that the summer hordes had returned to their inland lives, it was a pleasure to drink in all the quaint cuteness without sugar-mad kids dashing across her path.

Halloween must bring an influx of visitors, though, because most of the touristy shops were still open: The Mermaid's Cave Gift shop, Skee-Ball Madness Arcade, Sea Visions Art Gallery, Gelateria Paradiso, and one she hadn't noticed on her last trip: Madame Zora's Psychic Emporium. She'd have to check it out later, maybe bring Liv a crystal or two for her woo-woo meditations.

Addy forced her tense shoulders to relax. If she could handle all the other shitty cards life had dealt her, she could damn well quit whining and make the most of a week at the shore. Watching Snoot run on the beach would be fun. After six years of combat duty, he deserved to use his expertly trained sniffer on something less dangerous than IEDs.

As she turned down Narwhal Lane, Snoot perked up and thrust his nose through the open window to drink in the sea air.

"Smells good, doesn't it? Let's see, 128, 132…This is us, bud. Home sweet home for the next seven days."

Beach cottages didn't come cuter than this one: cedar shingles, a covered porch with an ocean-blue railing, a sandy front yard beneath sprawling, wind-sculpted madrona trees, kitschy garden sculptures and bird feeders, and a by-God hammock big enough for two, perfect for daydreaming.

"Well, at least we'll be comfortable in our solitude." As soon as she unfastened Snoot's harness, he sprang out and put his nose to the ground. Tail wagging, he snuffled through every inch of the front yard.

For the moment, Addy left the luggage in the open trunk and eased herself into the hammock. She gave an experimental push with her toe, and the canvas began to sway.

"Well, universe," she asked the cloud-dotted sky, "what's it gonna be? Another tour of duty, or do I slink back to Bumfuck, Nebraska?"

No answer came—except a soft whine at her elbow. Snoot gazed at her, his liquid brown eyes so full of concern she had to smile.

She patted the hammock. "Come on, boy."

He hopped up and nestled against her side with a contented doggy sigh. Addy stroked his thick brown fur. Mom would hate Snoot, would refuse him entry into her overstuffed house. Hell, she'd probably give him a swift kick when Addy's back was turned.

One more reason to avoid her childhood hometown.

But it would take a helluva long list to outweigh the most important reason tugging her back, the force that had driven her life for the past eleven years.

Duty.

Chapter Two

♥

Kieran Gallagher propped his boots on the metal railing atop Gull's Point Lighthouse and slurped his tea—strong, dark Irish breakfast brew, none of that wimpy supermarket swill. In most ways, he'd long ago adapted to life in the States, but a proper morning cuppa was sacrosanct, ditto a proper full Irish breakfast—minus the black pudding, nearly impossible to find on the Washington coast. He'd tried making that from scratch once, and it took days to get the burnt grease smell out of his cottage.

No bad smells today, though, especially at this early hour, when wisps of mist clung to the shoreline and a bracing breeze ruffled his beard. This was his favorite time of day. The lighthouse didn't officially open until ten, giving him a few precious hours to drink in the view, breathe the crisp sea air, and let his thoughts roll by unheeded. His therapist called it meditation, but to Kieran, it was simply the art of *being*. Learning this skill had saved his sanity—and probably his life.

Down on the beach, a dog raced along the waterline, a comically large stick in its jaws. The big brown pup sprinted in joyful figure eights, kicking up puffs of sand, then dashed back to its human—a woman with dark hair, dressed for a blustery autumn day in a windbreaker and jeans, with sandy runners on her feet.

Intrigued, Kieran leaned over the gallery railing for a closer look. He'd met most of the locals in Trappers Cove, but he didn't recognize this one.

The dog dropped its stick at her feet. Moving with relaxed grace, she picked it up and flung it far, sailing end over end.

Maybe he should get a dog of his own, another warm creature to keep him company during his solitary nights. Not that he craved much interaction after a long day of entertaining tourists, but dogs are simple, undemanding souls. Empathetic, too, though he'd probably terrify the poor beast when he bolted upright in bed, screaming, "Get to the lifeboats!"

The woman's laugh carried on the wind, a mellow, musical sound.

Maybe he should get one of those too—a proper girlfriend to share his cozy cottage at the base of the lighthouse. Since that horrible day, he limited his encounters with women to harmless flirtation and the occasional services of a sex worker. Why get attached to someone who'd inevitably flee when the terror came back?

And it always came back.

So the lighthouse keeper's cottage remained his alone, though many a pretty tourist had exclaimed how she'd loooove to live there. Technically, he was a park ranger, since all the Washington lighthouses had been automated in the seventies, but everyone in town still referred to him as the keeper.

Pretty sweet deal: a job where he could indulge his Irish talent for storytelling, and a home he didn't have to share with dozens of bunkmates. Just himself, the surf's soft whisper, and the occasional visit from a hundred-year-old ghost—much less scary than the hauntings in his head.

A bark rang out from nearby. He rose to his feet and peered down the footpath winding through the dunes. Sure enough, the woman and dog were heading his way. She kept up a steady patter of one-sided conversation, something about...

No, he couldn't have heard that right. Sounded like she said, "Bumfuck."

When she stepped over the chain closing off the parking lot, he cupped a hand to his mouth. "Ahoy, miss."

She jumped backward a good meter and clapped her hand over her heart—not the effect he was hoping for, especially from such a lovely visitor. Even from this height, he was struck by her shining dark hair and bright eyes. Too bad he couldn't make out their color.

"Good morning," she replied when she'd recovered her composure.

He'd been about to tell her the park didn't open until ten o'clock, but a playful notion nudged different words from his lips. "Care for a tour?"

Pale neck arched, she stared up at him, probably trying to decide if he was trustworthy. "I'm afraid my dog couldn't make the climb."

"Hang on. I'll be right down."

As his footfalls clanged on the spiral metal staircase, he chuckled at his own impulsivity. Something about this visitor and her pup intrigued him. And after a crucial hunch saved his life, he'd learned to respect inner nudges like this one.

If nothing else, he'd pet a cute dog and discover the color of the woman's eyes, information that suddenly seemed very important.

When he flung open the lighthouse door, they were still there. The woman crouched to rub the dog's belly. Tongue lolling, the beast wriggled and panted in canine glee.

"Top o' the mornin' to ya both." Laying the Irish accent on thick usually charmed the ladies—and he found himself particularly interested in charming this one.

The beauty laughed and pushed to her feet. "Is that accent for real?"

Green eyes, pale and glittering like the sea over a sand shoal, scanned him from head to toe before narrowing. She wrinkled her pointy, freckle-dusted nose and swiped a hank of nearly black hair from her forehead.

"As real as my beard, darlin'," he assured her, "and if you're not Irish too, I'm not standing here before you."

"What makes you say that?" She crossed her arms, clearly not buying his blarney. Her dog, however, showed no such mistrust. Despite his grizzled snout, he picked up his oversize stick and dropped it at Kieran's feet, his fat tail wagging with all the enthusiasm of a puppy.

"Because you're the very picture of a Black Irish beauty. May I?" He gestured toward the stick, and when the woman nodded, flung to the far side of the parking lot. The dog tore after it, barking joyfully.

He thrust out his hand. "Kieran Gallagher, lighthouse keeper and teller of tall tales, at your service."

The flicker of a smile warmed her expression as she slid her hand into his. "Addy Connor. Pleased to meet you Kieran."

"Irish name. I knew it. Where's your family from?"

That bewitching smile tilted into a smirk. "Bumfuck, Nebraska."

He spluttered a laugh. So he had heard correctly.

"Actually, it's Smithsville, but same difference. And you?"

"Well, I've been in Trappers Cove for a while now, but originally, I'm from your sister city, Ballygobackwards, Ireland."

She had the loveliest laughter, musical and low. "I like your version better. Let me guess—a small farm town where nothing much happens, and people are all up in each other's private business?"

"Accurate. And yours?"

"The same."

The dog returned, his wagging tail well peppered with marram grass seeds.

"Sorry about that." Kieran stooped to pluck the seeds from the dog's fur. "What's your name, fella?"

"It's Snoot." When Addy crouched to join him, her knee bumped into his, sending a spark of awareness over his skin.

Living up to his name, the dog gave Kieran a thorough sniff, then nudged his head into Kieran's palm.

"I've never met a Snoot before." While petting the pup, his hand brushed Addy's, and damn if another electric thrill didn't zing his nerves.

"His previous owner named him." When he raised an eyebrow, she added, "He was an Army explosives detection K9."

"Ah." He nodded. "A very skilled snoot indeed."

At the mention of his name, the pup tried to crawl into Kieran's lap, knocking him onto his bum.

"Easy, bud." Addy grabbed the dog's collar, but the beast was determined to give Kieran a tongue bath.

"Snoot, leave it." Her tone was stern now, and the dog immediately obeyed, sitting at her feet and gazing at her with rapt attention.

"Good boy." She gave his head a pat. "Well, we'd better move along."

"You've come all this way and don't want a tour?" Kieran hooked a thumb over his shoulder toward the lighthouse tower.

"Up there? The vet says he should avoid stairs, so..."

"Not a problem. I'll carry him. Come on, pal."

Tail wagging, the dog trotted after him, and after an audible scoff, so did his owner.

Kieran opened the door and began his well-rehearsed patter. "Welcome to Gull's Point historic lighthouse. Dating from 1894, it helped sailors navigate the treacherous waters at the mouth of the Columbia River, and—"

"Don't we need a ticket?"

"Consider it a veterans' discount." He flipped a switch, illuminating the information plaques that showed the building's structure and history. "Over here you'll see trinkets left behind by the former lighthouse keepers: spy glasses, logbooks, snuff tins." He tapped the glass. "Here's my favorite—a racy novel from the 1920s."

While Addy bent to examine *Lady Donatella's Gardener,* Kieran examined her. Lithe, graceful, with threads of silver wound through her wavy dark hair. The hand she held those tresses back with had short, unpainted fingernails. Her casual, outdoorsy clothing revealed nothing about her background. He'd have to tease that information out of her, and he only had a brief time to do so.

"Care to go up? It's a bit of a climb, but I promise, the view is worth the effort."

She nibbled her full lower lip before giving a crisp nod. "Why not?"

"Right. Up we go, doggo." He scooped the Labrador into his arms and tilted his chin toward the spiral staircase. "Ladies first."

She flashed a knowing grin over her shoulder and started up, fully aware of his intention to gawk at her arse. And what a fine view it was, curvy and firm, muscles clenching with each step. Good thing his hands were full with fifty-plus pounds of panting pup, lest they be tempted to stray where they weren't invited.

And what would it take to get an invitation from the lady?

Funny, since coming to this beach town five years ago, he hadn't felt compelled to extend a woman's acquaintance beyond the half-hour lighthouse tour. Easier to manage his own darkness without having to don a happy face for a ladylove. But after just ten minutes with Addy, he was already dreading the moment she waved goodbye.

They stopped at each level so he could present, and Snoot could sniff, the storerooms, the keeper's sleeping quarters, and the equipment room.

"Do you live up here?" she asked, eyeing the stiff, narrow cot.

"Thankfully, no. I'm in the little cottage at the base."

"But you make the climb every day?"

"At least twenty times."

And damn if her gaze didn't skim down his body, lingering on his thighs. He bit back a grin.

"Probably more effective than running on the beach."

"Is that what you do to keep so fit?" he asked.

She flashed a tilted grin and shrugged one shoulder. "I don't get the chance very often. Mostly, I run around the base."

"That military fort up north?"

"Joint Base Lewis-McChord, yeah."

Not inclined to give up personal details easily, was she? He sat on the cot, and Snoot immediately hopped up beside him and nestled against his thigh.

"You're a soldier, then?" he asked, stroking the dog's thick fur.

She turned away to examine a row of old tintypes on the wall, faded images of solemn-faced lighthouse keepers and their sturdy wives.

"Listen, miss, if you'd rather I not ask personal questions, I'll bite my tongue and get on with the tour. But I enjoy getting to know my visitors." He raised his palms in a placating gesture. "I promise, I mean you no harm."

Her expression softened. "It's fine. It's just that—" She sighed. "When I tell people what I do for a living, they tend to ask a lot of questions. Sometimes, it's nice to be anonymous, you know?"

Was she some kind of spy or special ops assassin? Images of sexy, bad-ass movie heroines dazzled his imagination, but he tamped down his curiosity. "Sure, of course. Everyone's entitled to a few secrets."

And keeping his ugly secret from her was his only chance to enjoy her company a little longer. Once women found out about the disaster and its aftermath, they inevitably bailed.

"Thanks for understanding." She crossed the narrow room and sat beside him on the squeaky cot. Sandwiched between them, the dog thumped the mattress with his tail and laid his head on her lap, eyeing Addy with heart-melting adoration. She absently stroked his fur and stared off into the distance.

"Most people wouldn't thrive in this kind of isolation." She nudged his shoulder with hers. "Do you?"

"Ah, who's asking questions now?" he teased.

"Sorry, that was too personal, wasn't it?" Her gaze dropped. "This is my week for asking hard questions, I guess. I find myself at a turning point, and there's a lot I need to figure out pretty quickly."

"Like whether you enjoy isolation?"

"Sort of. And whether I could thrive in a small town."

"Small like Bumfuck, or like Trappers Cove?"

"Are they that different?"

"Very much so." He slapped his thighs and pushed to his feet. "Well, Ms. Mystery, are you ready to go up topside?"

"Lead on, Lighthouse Keeper."

At the top of the final staircase, Kieran opened the heavy metal door while Addy clipped the dog's leash to his collar. "Heel, Snoot."

Unlike many visitors, this beauty displayed not the least hesitation stepping onto the platform. And like the well-trained soldier he was, the dog glued himself to her side, calm despite the swooping seagulls overhead, and contented himself with sniffing the wind that lifted his mistress's hair.

It was always interesting to see how people reacted to the view up here. Some plastered themselves to the sturdy wall, jaws tight, lips bloodless. Some giggled, made giddy by the height. Some winced at the wind's power. But not secretive Addy. She rested her hands lightly on the railing and slowly scanned the horizon.

"Wow," she said at last, "I was about to turn back when Snoot tugged me toward this place. It's..." She sighed through a misty smile. "What an amazing view. Makes me feel like I'm above it all, you know? All the petty day-to-day bullshit, the complications, the..." She trailed off, spread her arms wide, and closed her eyes. "The wind blows it all away."

Kieran stepped up beside her, awed by how perfectly she expressed the comfort he felt up here. "It's an excellent place to have a think."

She gifted him a brilliant smile. "You're a lucky man, Kieran Gallagher."

"I am today," he agreed, drinking in the sight of her—jade eyes shining, dark hair whipping in the wind.

She tossed off a laugh. "Are you flirting with me, sir?"

"Just a wee bit, ma'am. Do you mind?"

Her gaze held a playful twinkle. "I suppose not. What happens at the beach stays at the beach, right?"

He inched closer. "And how long might you be staying at the beach?"

"A week."

A grin stretched his lips. "You'll be here for Halloween, then. Might even see the ghost."

She rolled her eyes. "Pfft. Save your blarney for the tourists."

He gripped the railing, his hand mere inches from hers. "No blarney, my lovely skeptic. I doubted too, when I first arrived, but I've seen her with my own eyes and shivered at the sound of her voice."

She arched one dark eyebrow. "A talking ghost?"

"Mary Darrow, wife of Jonathan Darrow, captain of the Ivanova." He pointed to a rocky outcropping barely visible beneath the surf. "Her husband's vessel ran aground in 1822, returning from Alaska with a cargo of furs. I'm sure you've heard how treacherous these waters can be near the mouth of the Columbia. Everyone aboard perished. But when the moon is full, you can still see her, a ragged ship with glowing sails."

Okay, that part was a local legend—he'd yet to see a ghostly ship, and not for lack of trying.

"And down below," he pointed to the tower's base, "the captain's widow paces the shore, a spyglass in her hand, watching for her husband's return."

That part was real enough. The first time he'd seen the mournful spirit, he'd stood frozen in place as the misty outline solidified into a woman with upswept hair and long, wind-blown skirts, a lantern in one hand and an old-fashioned spy glass in the other. Movie ghosts floated gracefully, but this phantom's movements were jerky and agitated as she searched the horizon.

And when she turned to look right at him, a wave of sadness chilled him to the marrow.

"Jonathan?" she cried, her anxious voice somehow ringing inside his skull. Her dark eyes wide, she stepped toward him. Panicked, he stumbled backward, and when he looked again, she was gone.

Since then, he'd seen her a dozen times, usually from the safety of the lighthouse gallery. Poor, restless spirit, endlessly searching for her lost love.

Addy's shoulders rose and fell on a deep inhalation. "A ghost, huh? I carry around a lot of those."

Well, shite, he'd hoped to entice her into another visit, and instead he'd brought up bad memories.

Down below, a minivan rolled into the parking lot and disgorged two men and four stair-step children. An SUV followed, and a Tesla.

Kieran rubbed his palms together. "Time to get to work. Tell you what, Ms. Addy—we're expecting clear skies tonight. Full moon too. I'm making the best pumpkin soup you've ever tasted, and a pie from apples grown right there." He pointed over his shoulder toward Oscar and Evelyn's orchard. "There'll be plenty to share if you care to come by and watch for the White Widow. Or we can stay inside if that doesn't appeal to your sense of adventure."

His gamble paid off, judging by the sparkle in her smile.

"Sense of adventure, eh? I used to have one of those." She crouched to scratch her dog's jaw. "What do you say, Snoot? Do we trust this guy?"

Tongue lolling, the Lab leaned against Kieran's leg and gave a happy doggy groan.

"Seems you've made a friend, Keeper. All righty then—I guess we'll see you tonight."

"Excellent. Around six?" That'd give him time to defrost the soup he'd made last week after going nuts at the Trappers Cove farmers market—and bake one of the pies he'd frozen. Thanking the heavens for his foresight, he scooped the pup into his arms. "Down we go, buddy."

Addy's eyebrows flicked up. "After you, Keeper Kieran."

Oho, he liked the sound of that—and the idea she might be checking out his rear view as well.

His luck was definitely looking up.

At the base of the stairs, he bent to ruffle the dog's fur and accept a slobbery kiss.

"Snoot, don't be gross," she admonished and gripped the beast's collar to pull him away. "Sorry."

He chuckled. "I'll take my kisses where I can get them."

And damn if she didn't bite her lip again, tempering a saucy grin. "No promises, but if your apple pie is good enough, you might get a few more."

Addy reattached the dog's leash and sashayed toward the beach, her trim hips swaying.

Kieran raised his eyes heavenward. "Whatever angel's watching out for me, thank you."

Chapter Three

♥

Addy closed her paperback mystery, gazed up at the swaying branches above her comfy hammock, and smiled around a contented sigh. Though she was no closer to deciding what to do about her mom, her career, all of it, Liv's advice rang true. This funky little beach town gave her space to breathe and let her ideas percolate. Not to mention how happy Snoot seemed here. Sprawled beneath her hammock, he lifted his head now and then to sniff the briny breeze.

A few more days like this, and she'd have it all figured out. In the meantime, she'd enjoy this perfectly cool, sunny weather, this perfectly cozy cottage, this perfect peace.

After their morning beach walk and encounter with the hunky, flirtatious lighthouse keeper, she'd devoured a huge breakfast at Cassie's Coastal Café, then strolled through the shops on the west side of Main Street, netting some sea-mineral bath bombs, a scarf in ocean hues, and a stack of paperbacks from Bookish, the cute bookshop near the end of the touristy half mile. Souvenir Galaxy and the hippie crystal shop could wait until tomorrow. Or the next day.

How wonderful not to be in a hurry for once! No pager buzzing in her pocket, no post-op check-ins and electronic paperwork, no mountain of work emails...

Her phone pinged. Acting on autopilot, she pulled it from her pocket. And just like that, her perfect peace imploded.

Colonel Magda Okafor, the commander of Madigan Army Medical Center, wouldn't interrupt Addy's leave if it weren't urgent. Liv would scold her for answering, but when duty calls...

"Ma'am?"

"Drop the formality, Addy." Her boss's voice sounded brittle and exhausted. "I'm sorry to bother you, but the brass is on my ass about staffing. I'm afraid I'll need your decision by the first of the month."

"But that's—" Addy double-checked her phone calendar.

"The day after Halloween. And you'll still be on leave. I know, Addy, and I hate to put this kind of pressure on you, but I'm up against the wall. By COB next Friday, I have to submit my staffing plan. You know how it is—lots of folks retire at the end of the calendar year, take terminal leave, blah blah blah. I'd hoped I could give you more time, but I just can't."

A sudden heaviness weighed Addy's limbs as she ended the call and sank back into the hammock. She'd thought she had until the end of November to decide whether to extend her Army service for another term. Making big life decisions quickly had never been her forte, and now, she had one week to choose: more of the same? Or play the dutiful daughter and return to a town she hated? Or something else—as if she had any frickin' idea what that might be.

"Arrgh. This was supposed to be a vacation." Addy doubled over and hugged her roiling middle.

Snoot's cold, damp nose prodded her palm.

"I'm okay, buddy." She ruffled his thick fur. "Actually, we both know that's a lie, but life goes on, whether we're ready or not, right?"

His soul-searching gaze coaxed a smile to her lips. "What do you say we go for a sniff on the beach?"

Snoot whuffed his excitement and bounced on his front paws.

Rising with a groan, Addy went inside to gather the scent tins she'd learned how to use at the military K-9 adoption program. Working dogs need a job to stay healthy and happy, the trainer had explained, and since Snoot's job was scent detection, she enriched their walks by hiding targets for him to find—cotton balls soaked with anise or clove. He adored the challenge, and she enjoyed watching his joyful, tail-whipping searches.

One of the program's teachers had suggested she train Snoot for search and rescue work. Addy loved the idea, but with her current schedule, she just couldn't spare the time. Hell, she hardly had time to think, much less develop a new passion.

She forced her tense shoulders down and grabbed Snoot's leash. "It's too beautiful a day to spiral into negativity—and we have a date tonight!"

After their romp on the beach, Addy returned to her cottage windblown, sun-pinked, and lighter of spirit. How incredibly lucky she was to be stationed within driving distance of such a gorgeous place. If she opted for another tour in the Army Medical Corps, chances were slim she'd get an assignment this close to the coast. And if she went back to her childhood home, the only ocean in sight would be a sea of soybean plants. Ugh.

"What would it be like to live here and walk on the beach whenever I please?" she asked her reflection as she dressed for her dinner date with Kieran. The sun had coaxed even more freckles across the bridge of her nose. She reached for her cosmetic bag, then thought better of it. "Take me as I am or..." She fastened her new earrings—silver dangles with tiny citrine stones. "Or don't shake my peach tree. Is that how it goes, bud?"

From his cushion at the foot of her bed, Snoot gave a whuff of agreement.

She dug through her suitcase for a scarf to complement her pale green cashmere sweater. "I mean, it's not like I'll ever see this guy again."

The dog thumped his tail on the cushion.

"Besides, who needs a boyfriend when I've got the best boy in the world?" She crouched to cup his chocolate brown face in both hands and smooch his broad forehead. Immediately, he flopped over for a belly rub.

While she skritched his soft fur, her thoughts drifted back to the lighthouse keeper and how sweet he'd been with Snoot. It wasn't like her to accept a spontaneous date. Usually, she carefully vetted her dates before agreeing to meet. Come to think of it, better give someone a heads-up before meeting up with a near stranger.

She typed a quick text to Liv.

> **How's it going with the Stryker Brigade?**

Her friend's answer came quickly.

> **Rough. Had to go to Supply for more Kleenex. Twice.**

> **Ah, Liv, I'm sorry. I should've stayed to help.**

Addy started to type a message about Col. Okafor's news, then erased it. Her friend was dealing with enough stress as it was. Besides, what could Liv do about a staffing issue?

> **Bullshit, missy. You did your part. Now go spoil your overworked ass. Self-care, darling.**

> **Does a date count?**

A string of emojis followed: a gawking face, a grinning one, and a thumbs up. And then an eggplant.

> **Whoa now, I just met the guy. In case he turns out to be a serial killer, I'll be at Gull's Point Lighthouse with Kieran Gallagher.**

She'd memorized the spelling from his uniform nametag.

> **If you don't text by midnight, I'll send the National Guard.**

Midnight? The last time she'd stayed up that late was New Year's Eve at the Officers Club.

> **I'll text by ten. Love you, sis.**

Liv's answer: a kiss-blowing emoji.

Eggplant, huh? Could she justify a quick tumble with a willing stranger as self-care? Because Kieran the keeper was mighty tempting.

Snoot tugged hard on the leash, eager to return to his new friend. Or maybe it was just the delicious cooking smells drifting from the stone cottage that fueled his hurry.

When they reached the door, Snoot dropped onto the ground, his trained response to finding a scent target. Weird.

"Is this guy cooking up explosives, bud?" She gave his head a scratch and knocked on the door, which immediately opened to reveal Kieran in a canvas apron that read *Kiss the Cook* and a faded lobster-claw oven mitt.

Tail wagging like a windshield wiper on overdrive, Snoot sprang up and planted his feet on Kieran's stomach.

"Sorry. Down, Snoot." The dog obediently sat beside her and whimpered, practically vibrating with joy.

If she had a tail, she'd wag it too. *Hunky* was inadequate to describe their host. He'd looked pretty damn sexy in his crisp park ranger uniform, but in snug, worn jeans and a dark green

Henley, sleeves pushed up to the elbows to reveal powerful, copper-dusted forearms? Yowza!

She yanked her gaze away from forearm heaven toward his face but got stuck at the vee of russet chest hair curling from the opening in his shirt.

Clearly, Liv was right. Her last sexual encounter was ages ago, and you can only squash a healthy libido for so long.

"You came!" Laugh lines crinkled the corners of his bright hazel eyes, cognac brown with glints of green and gold. His short, silver-sprinkled beard framed plump lips stretched in a welcoming smile.

She knew it was rude, but she couldn't help gawking at his broad shoulders, well-muscled chest, and sturdy thighs. Old-fashioned woolen slippers covered his enormous feet. Cozy, cute, and delectably male. Powerful stuff!

Addy shuffled her sand-dusted sneakers on his welcome mat and held out the potted mini-ivy plant she'd picked up at the Main Street Food Co-op. "Thanks for having me."

"How thoughtful." He cupped her elbow and pulled her inside, inclining his head toward a bench beside the door. "Hope you don't mind taking off your shoes. Sand gets everywhere, you know." With his slippered foot, he nudged forward a wicker basket filled with cloth slippers of various sizes. "My sister sent these for guests."

She toed off her sneakers and chose a pair, noting the tatami insole. "Japanese slippers from an Irish sister?"

He chuckled, a deep, rumbly sound that warmed her better than the flames crackling in the stone hearth. "We're a far-flung family. Fiona lives in Kyoto. Maeve is in Switzerland, Seamus is in Toronto, and I'm here. Only Aisling stayed in Ireland."

"Your parents must miss you very much."

His handsome face screwed into a grimace. "They're gone."

Okaaay, best to leave that touchy subject alone. Seems they had that in common—prickly relationships with their families.

"May I, Mr. Snoot?" Kieran grabbed a towel and crouched to rub the sand from Snoot's fur—a task the dog made easier by sprawling on his back. The smile Kieran flashed up at her ignited a whole squadron of fireflies in her belly.

He pushed to his feet. "Hope you don't have a problem with dairy. There's cream in the soup and plenty of cheese." He rubbed his nose and cracked a boyish grin. "I went a little mad at the farmer's market."

"Are you kidding? I'd live on cheese if I could." She sniffed the air. "Smells delicious."

With his hand on the small of her back, a courtly gesture that sent tingles up her spine, he led her to a corner table set for two. She took a seat on the padded bench.

While Kieran gathered dishes and serving utensils, she checked out his quaint, cozy home. Hardwood floors polished to a high gloss, braided rugs in front of the stone fireplace and beneath the dining table, lots of old-timey photos and prints on the white-paneled walls, and—an incongruous but charming touch—trailing ivy in seventies-style macrame plant hangers. Old-fashioned with a hippie twist, comfy and welcoming.

Yum.

"I've got cider from the Salty Dog Brewery. It's—" Kieran lifted a dark-brown growler and squinted at the label. "Spiced pear."

"Sounds delish, thanks."

He poured her a glass before filling his own glass with tap water. Huh. Was he in recovery?

He caught her sideways glance at his drink. "I do better without alcohol." The corners of his full mouth quirked upward. "Despite the stereotype, not all Irishmen are lushes."

"Of course they aren't." Her cheeks heated.

Kieran carried an old-fashioned soup tureen to the table, along with a basket of crusty peasant bread, a crock of butter, a green salad, and three kinds of artisanal cheese.

Addy surveyed the feast and gave a low whistle. "Wow. Were you a chef before you became a lighthouse keeper?"

He threw his head back and laughed, displaying the strong column of his throat—yet another delicious detail she'd love to explore.

Yikes, what was up with this sudden libido spike? She'd like to blame the cider, but she'd yet to taste a drop.

"My job was about as far away from chefing as you can get." He ladled soup into her bowl, then passed a small dish of pumpkin seeds to sprinkle on top. "Though I did take my turn cooking for the crew."

"What kind of crew?" She reached for the bread. "Let me guess—you were a firefighter?"

Kieran flinched, and his lips thinned into a tight line, though he quickly hid his reaction behind a teasing smile. "Ah, ah, ah." He slathered his slice with butter. "You first."

Well, poop. She'd hoped to dance around that topic. Stalling, she dipped her spoon into the soup and brought it to her lips, then moaned as rich, pumpkin-y velvet slid over her tongue.

Kieran chuckled around his own spoonful. "It's okay if you don't want to talk about your work. I'm interested in you, Addy, not your resume."

Well, their easy rapport was nice while it lasted. She gripped her spoon tighter and braced herself for the usual awkwardness. "I'm a surgeon. In the Army."

His eyebrows shot up. "That would not have been my first guess."

"Oh?" She gave him a playful grin. "What would you have guessed?"

He stroked his beard, kindling her desire to do the same. "Something outdoorsy, I'd think. But working with people.

You have an air of kindness about you. I see it in the way you look out for Snoot."

At the mention of his name, the dog set his chin on her knee and gazed up adoringly. Addy patted his broad head. "Well, who could meet this fella and not fall in love?"

"Compassionate," Kieran continued, "that's the word I want. I'd expect a surgeon to be more..." He scrunched his lips to the side.

"Detached? Clinical?" She tore off another chunk of bread. "I am, when I need to be. When you're wrist-deep in some-one's belly, you can't afford to get emotional about it."

"I'll bet that takes a toll on someone like you."

She sighed. "It does."

Giving in to the urge to touch him, she patted Kieran's thick forearm. "Maybe I should become a park ranger."

"Comin' for my job, are you? I'll warn you, it involves car-rying heavy dogs up the stairs."

Oh, Liv would like this guy. He had her best friend's knack for seeing through defenses and pretenses, right to the beating heart of the matter—not that she was pretending with Kieran. Why should she? After this week, she'd never see him again, and that made him a safe confidante for all her messy issues. For some strange reason, he seemed content to listen. In fact, he seemed downright fascinated. Maybe that was just a front designed to get her in bed.

And maybe she was perfectly fine with that.

Chapter Four

♥

Kieran leaned onto his elbows and placed his big, work-roughened hand on hers. "So, a pretty surgeon and her faithful dog come to my lighthouse in search of..." His crooked smile was the most disarming, seductive thing Addy had seen—and felt—in a very long time.

She turned her hand palm to palm with his. "I find myself at a crossroads, and there's a lot I need to figure out pretty quickly."

"Personal stuff, or job stuff?"

"Both."

When she hesitated, chewing her lip, he added, "I've found that saying the painful stuff out loud can help."

"Pretty wise, aren't you?" But was he patient enough to wade through the quagmire that was her life right now? And did she have the fortitude to lay it all out for him?

"Any wisdom I may have, I came by it the hard way." He leaned onto his elbows and rested his chin on his knuckles. "Here's your chance to unburden yourself to a sympathetic stranger with absolutely no skin in the game."

Why did he have to mention skin? Now she was picturing his. Was it freckled all over, or pale and creamy where the sun didn't touch him?

Stalling, she mopped up the last of her soup with a hunk of bread and popped it into her mouth.

Kieran's gaze never faltered.

"Well," she began, "I have three choices: Extend my military service. I have eleven years in, and I'll be eligible for full retirement after twenty."

"You enjoy serving your country?"

"I do." At least she could say that with complete honesty. "In the Army, I've found something I couldn't find back home."

"In Bumfuck, Nebraska?"

She spluttered a laugh. "You have an excellent memory."

"When the subject interests me." He quirked an eyebrow. "So, what couldn't you find at home?"

Though she hated to admit it, Kieran was right. Talking it out with a stranger really did help because his opinion of her ultimately didn't matter, even if she liked him.

For once, she had zero excuses to be less than completely honest.

"In the Army, I found a sense of belonging. Acknowledgement of my strengths. Feeling like my contribution matters."

"Everyone needs that."

"And do you get a sense of belonging here?"

His smile widened. "I do indeed. Trappers Cove people are kind. They look out for each other. Sure, there's some small-town gossip, sometimes a little too much interference in each other's business, but it comes from a place of caring." He rubbed his thumb over his bottom lip, his gaze far away. "Never got that from my family of origin."

"Family of origin? Sounds like therapy-speak."

A wry smile curved his mouth. "It is. Took me a while to be comfortable admitting that, but here we are." He cut a slice of cheese, then nudged the plate toward her. "So, you get what you need from the military?"

"I do." She helped herself to creamy cheddar flecked with chives, so good she had to close her eyes and let out a moan.

When she opened them again, Kieran's gaze was riveted on her mouth.

She dabbed her lips with her napkin. "As horrible as it was working in a combat zone, the experience bonded us. No matter what happens, the people I served with will always be my family."

"And will that still be true if you leave the military?"

"I guess. But I'd feel like I'm letting them down." She ripped off another hunk of bread. "Brothers and sisters in arms, and all that."

Kieran's almost-too-big-to-be-real hand gave her wrist a gentle squeeze. "You know, there were a lot of veterans in my therapy group. That camaraderie you speak of doesn't go away just because they no longer wear a uniform."

"That's good to hear." Pretty much anything he wanted to say in that musical Irish accent was good to hear, and she fought to focus on his actual words.

With perfectly awful timing, her phone buzzed with an incoming message.

She gave him a sheepish grin. "Sorry, this might be work."

"No problem." With an easy smile, he rose and cleared away the dishes, closely tailed by Snoot. Kieran cut a sliver of cheese and held it up for Addy's permission.

Why not? Her buddy had been good as gold throughout their meal and deserved a treat.

While Kieran washed up and Snoot snapped up the cheese, Addy checked her phone. Ugh.

Not from work, but from her cousin Caitlynn. If not for her mom's ill health, she'd have silenced the family group chat long ago.

> **Listen, Miss Snootypants, your mama needs you. Quit being selfish. Grow up and pay her back for everything she's done for you.**

Addy's face flushed. *Everything she's done for me? That's a laugh.*

From the first time she'd expressed an interest in college, her mother's sparse support shriveled into pursed-mouth disproval and snide comments about putting on airs. When Addy announced her acceptance into the Army's Health Professions Scholarship Program, you'd think she'd shit on the grave of every ancestor in Smithsville's Blessed Acres Cemetery.

The Connor clan simply could not conceive of a life worth living beyond shouting distance of each other's backyards. Never mind the good Addy did with her surgical skills. Never mind the money she dutifully sent home to support her mother, though she suspected much of it ended up in her siblings' wallets.

"Joining the Army?" Mama had spat out as Addy packed for Officer Basic Military Training. "That's the most ridiculous thing I've ever heard. You're just running away from your responsibilities. I don't see why you can't find a nice man and settle down right here. Guess blood means nothing to you."

Blood—hah! Addy had seen more blood than her sheltered family could imagine. She'd saved countless lives, but that didn't matter to any of them because their tiny town was the center of the freakin' universe.

With a disgusted tsk, she pocketed her phone.

Kieran returned with steaming mugs of tea that smelled like spice and apples. "Bad news?"

"Family stuff. It can wait."

"Good." He sat on the bench and scooted a little closer. "So, you've listed the pros of staying in the military. What about the cons?"

Addy winced and squirmed in her seat. "Listen, I…"

Kieran raised his palms. "It's none of my business, Doc, but you know what they say about ripping off the Band-aid." He nudged her arm. "Whatever you share tonight doesn't leave this room."

Funny how a lighthouse keeper made a better therapist than the highly qualified psychologist assigned to her case.

She extended her pinkie. "You swear?"

"On everything that's good and holy." He hooked his little finger through hers, lifted her hand to his mouth, and brushed his soft lips across her knuckles.

Flushed with pleasure from head to toe, she cleared her throat to wipe the wobble from her voice, reminding herself she'd come to Trappers Cove to figure out her life, not to bed an extremely hot Irishman.

"The downside is war. After two tours in a combat zone, they probably won't deploy me again, but you never know. And that experience was—" Her skin pebbled into goose-bumps. "Horrible. Terrifying. The hardest thing I've ever done."

Kieran's gaze remained steady—not the tiniest flicker of *"What the hell am I getting into with this woman?"*

Heartened by his quiet interest, she continued. "I've been in therapy ever since returning from my second tour in Afghanistan, and it's not helping much. I've been using my duties as an excuse to avoid doing the hard emotional work I need, and I'm starting to..." She rotated her wrist as she searched for the right words. "Fray, I guess. Like a worn-out rope that's about to snap."

He nodded slowly. "And leaving the military would give you the chance to..." He repeated her gesture.

"The chance to breathe. Maybe if I don't spend every day surrounded by reminders of war, I'll find peace."

"Hmm." Holding her gaze, he nibbled his lip for a moment before giving his head a tiny shake. "You mentioned three choices. What's the second?"

She slumped against the seatback. "Moving home to a small rural town in the middle of, well, cornfields. And soybeans. And probably more cows than people."

His eyes narrowed. "You're talking about your family's home, Addy. Where's your home?"

"That's a damn good question." She huffed a laugh. "For the past eleven years, home has been wherever the Army sent me."

"You like Washington?"

"Very much." She gazed past his broad shoulder to the window beyond, where the shadows of pine branches danced in the coastal wind. "It's so green. And people are tolerant here, not always trying to squish you into a box. Then there's the mountains, the ocean, excellent coffee..." Trouble was, one way or another, she'd be leaving this state soon.

Only a quick change of subject could save her from an embarrassing flood of tears.

"How did you end up here, Kieran?"

A shadow crossed his face. "Let's save that story for dessert. We can take our pie outside and watch for the ghost. Deal?"

Grinning, she leaned onto her elbows. "Evasive, aren't you?"

"Look who's talking. Don't think I didn't notice how you change the subject just as we're getting to the meat of your dilemma."

She laughed again. "Okay, okay. You sound like my friend Liv. She's a psychologist, and she never lets me wriggle out of hard conversations. In fact, she was supposed to be here to help me talk through all this, but..." she shrugged. "Duty calls."

Kieran's warm hazel eyes sparkled with humor. "Well then, 'tis a good thing you met me. So—option two is going to Nebraska because..."

"My mother is ailing—or so she says." The opening salvo of a headache throbbed behind her forehead. "She's only seventy-three and remarkably active for someone who claims she can't manage her affairs, but she insists I come take care of her."

"You're an only child, then?"

She snorted. "Half that tiny town is related to Mama. But I'm the only single female in my generation, so in their eyes, it's my job."

"Got it. The old crabs in a bucket mentality." His brogue thickened and took on a whiny tone. "You're no better than any of us, and don't you forget it." He laid his hand over hers and squeezed gently. "But you are, you know."

"I am what?"

"Better than them. And it's not because of your education or earning power or skills. It's because your heart and mind are open, and theirs are closed." He laced his fingers through hers, and pleasure flowed through her veins like honey.

"So, lovely Addy, why even consider living where you're not appreciated?"

"Duty." Her sigh emptied her lungs. "If I've endured two tours in a war zone, I should be able to handle a few years in a claustrophobic small town."

"And if she lives longer than that? The malicious ones often do. Spite keeps them going."

She growled her frustration. "But what kind of daughter refuses her sick, elderly mother? That's what it boils down to, even if she is mean as a snake."

Kieran folded his other hand around hers, surrounding her with warm strength. "She's got her guilt hooks into you good. So, option one: stay in the military. Option two: go home to Mama. Option three is…?"

She groaned and slumped onto the table. "I don't know."

He released her hand and rubbed soothing circles between her shoulder blades. "Someone with your qualifications must have lots of options. Why not find a job somewhere you'd like to live? You can finance your mother's care while the rest of the family looks after her."

"They'd hound me for being a disloyal daughter." Hell, they were already doing that. Had been for years, in fact.

Kieran smacked the table, shaking the dishes. "So feckin' what?"

Heart racing, Addy jolted upright. Immediately, Snoot was on his feet, growling low.

Kieran raised his hands in a placating gesture. "Apologies. That hit a nerve, but you don't deserve my anger." His shoulders slumped. "And the people who do are dead, so..." He pushed back from the table. "What do you say to hot apple pie and stargazing?"

Chapter Five

♥

Before taking their dessert outside, Kieran went to the cedar chest to gather warm woolen blankets, and sent up a silent prayer that Addy wouldn't ask him to start a fire. He and the lovely doctor were—his niece in Toronto would call it "vibing," and he was eager to explore this new connection, but open flames plus ocean view? That combination was still a bridge too far. It had taken him a full year of living in the cottage before he worked up the nerve to light the fireplace.

After years of therapy, he'd finally learned to maneuver around his triggers and sleep through the night—mostly. Okay, sometimes. But he was so much better than the jittery mess of a man who came to Trappers Cove in search of a fresh start. Adding a woman to the mix would require rethinking...well, pretty much everything. The delicate balance of his new life might topple if he attempted an actual relationship.

But with Addy, there was no danger of that, a thought that landed in his gut with a sickening thunk. Even if she gave him a tumble, she was only in town for a week, and she'd be leaving Washington soon. Seems he'd just met "the one who got away."

But she wasn't gone yet.

Arms loaded with blankets, he lowered the chest's lid, but it slipped from his fingers and slammed shut with a loud bang. Behind him, the dog yelped.

"Sorry, buddy. Clumsy of me." He turned to find Snoot under the dining table, huddled with his mistress, who crouched on her knees and clasped her hands over her nape as if shielding herself from falling debris. The Lab nuzzled her hair and whined.

"Jaysus," he murmured and dropped the blankets. Lowering himself to the floor, he crawled under the table, where the poor woman hunched, trembling like an aspen leaf.

"Addy, I'm sorry. I didn't mean to startle you. You're safe, I promise."

Slowly, cautiously, she unfolded and raised her head. Her gaze was haunted, her tear-streaked cheeks ashen.

"Hey now, it's okay." He gathered her into his arms and held her against his chest until she stopped shaking. Finally, she released a long, trembling breath. "Sorry, Kieran. I'm not usually this jumpy. Sometimes, it just sneaks up on me, you know?"

His poor heart squeezed like a fist. "PTSD, is it?"

Her chuckle rang brittle as glass. "Helluva way for you to find out."

He stroked her hair, pulled loose from its knot by the sudden scramble for shelter. "Fella in my therapy group reacted the same when the wind blew the door open."

"I'm being ridiculous," she muttered into his shoulder. "Startling like a scared rabbit. The combat soldiers I treated saw so much worse than I ever did. All I had to do was stitch up the aftermath." Her voice hitched as she fixed him with wide, glassy eyes. "But there were so many I couldn't save."

"Oh, darling." He hugged her tight and rested his cheek against her silky hair. She smelled of springtime, green and fresh and full of promise, but this delicate-seeming woman had endured horrors beyond his imagination. And considering his own trauma, that was saying quite a lot.

"Well, I'll let you in on a secret." He rocked her slowly, hoping the motion would settle her.

She gave a mighty sniffle. "What's that?"

"I have the same diagnosis."

She propped her chin on his chest and drilled him with her reddened, watery eyes. "What happened?"

"Oil rig fire. Lost some dear friends. Family, really." He tilted his head toward the door. "Come outside and I'll tell you my tale. What do you say?" A change of topic and a bit of soul-baring might soothe her crackling nerves. Not that he looked forward to prying the lid off that can of snakes, but she'd shared her own traumatic past. Fair's fair.

And if he was a hundred percent honest with himself, Addy's brave honesty made her the perfect person to open up to. The time had come to admit the truth he'd fought since quitting his therapy group—going it alone wasn't working.

"Damn it to hell and back." She wiped her eyes on her sleeve. "Way to make a good impression."

Chuckling, he pressed a kiss to her forehead. "I have nothing but high esteem for you, Addy." He scooted backward, got his feet under him, and extended his hand. "Shall we?"

He loaded a tray with two generous servings of warm apple pie, ceramic mugs, and a thermos of herbal tea, then draped a blanket around Addy's shoulders and folded the other over his arm.

As they made their way to the bench behind the lighthouse, Addy peered up at the tower and frowned. "Is that feeble light enough to warn ships?"

"Good thing it's not. Otherwise, we'd be besieged by bats and bugs." He set down the tray on a low table and pointed to a bright flash offshore. "This light is just for show. There's a series of beacons out there now. The waters at the mouth of the Columbia are too treacherous for one little lighthouse to be of much help."

"Ah." She settled onto the bench at the bluff's edge. "All the better for us, I suppose. So many stars!" She tilted her head back to drink it all in, exposing the pale, smooth arc of her throat.

Kieran bit his lower lip hard and fought the almost irresistible urge to kiss the satiny skin she'd bared.

A half-hour later, their pie devoured and their tea mugs empty, they sat side by side, each wrapped in blankets and watching the full moon's glow sprinkle diamonds across the waves.

When their companionable silence stretched into awkwardness, Kieran cleared his throat. "Right. Well, I promised you my story, if you're still up for it."

Addy's jade eyes glimmered with reflected moonlight. "It's okay if you don't want to tell me."

The compassion in her gaze gave him the strength to dive in. "It's never easy, but sharing with someone who's experienced something similar, it lightens the load, you know?"

"In that case, I'd be honored to hear it." Addy extricated her hand from her blanket cocoon and set it between them, facing up. He nestled his palm into her grip, relishing her warmth and steadiness.

"Right. Well, it was my third year of working the rigs out in the Gulf of Mexico. Great crew. Working together in close quarters, twelve-hour shifts, far from the comforts of home, we became like family to each other."

Though he was as fond of embellishing a story as any Irishman, that was no exaggeration. Out there on the rig, surrounded by choppy waters, battered by wind and rain and blazing sun, he and his crewmates shared every dream, every regret, every secret. Sure, they squabbled like brothers sometimes, but he'd trusted them with his very life.

"Wait, back up." She gave his hand a squeeze. "How did you end up on an oil rig in the Gulf? That's pretty damn far from Ireland."

Might as well share that bit of ugliness while he was at it. "After Mam died, Dad dove head-first into the bottle and never came out. Mean drunk. Took it out on his kids, so each of us fled as soon as we were of age. A cousin in Texas married a roughneck, and he got me the job. The money was good, and the camaraderie healed me—especially Jack Jefferson, our foreman." His lips stretched in a fond smile. "I needed a father figure, and he was kind to me. Whipped me into shape, you could say. Wise old fart, he was. Saw through my bluster and bullshit, right to my hurting heart." He stroked the back of Addy's hand with his thumb. "We need more of his sort in the world."

He fell into silence as flame-licked memories swirled, and once again he sent up a silent prayer that Jack didn't suffer. Why a great man like Jack was taken while he was spared remained the most baffling mystery of Kieran's life.

Addy nudged his shoulder with hers. "You want to stop there?"

Truth be told, he'd much rather keep the gory details locked down tight. But his therapist touted the benefits of—what was it called?—Cognitive Processing something or other. Talking it all out to keep it from festering.

Beyond that, Addy was hurting, and he felt a bone-deep need to help her. Call it kismet or cosmic guidance, this new connection vibrated with significance. They were kindred souls learning to live again after trauma.

Who knows, maybe he could even convince her to stick around. Trappers Cove was the most welcoming place he'd ever lived, and the town's hospital, really just a clinic, was chronically short of medical staff. He damn sure wouldn't mind seeing Addy on the other end of a stethoscope.

He refilled their mugs from the thermos. "I'll keep it short, because a night like this is too beautiful to spoil with ugly details. You see—" He shifted in his seat, searching for the right words. No use boring her with technicalities. "To drill into the sea floor, you've got to maintain a careful balance between gas pushing up and mud pushing down. When too much gas rises, we call it a 'kick,' and on the third of May six years ago, the earth gave us a mighty kick."

Before that day, he'd thought of Mother Nature as mostly benevolent, sometimes cranky, but on that bright morning, he'd learned what a vengeful bitch she could be.

"Natural gas is heavier than air, you see. It pooled around the derrick floor, and something ignited it. Probably static electricity. We'll never know for sure because the evidence burned and melted."

Addy inhaled sharply and tightened her grip. He raised her hand to his chest and pressed her palm over his heart.

"I should've been there at the detonation point. It was my turn to monitor the controls, but something—a weird hunch that crawled over my skin like ants—sent me back to my bunk belowdecks, convinced I'd forgotten something. When I came back topside, I heard an evil hiss that grew louder and louder. Now, there are lots of noises on an offshore rig—machinery, wind, crashing surf, shouting voices, but I'd never heard anything like this."

Even now, six years later, that ominous sizzle haunted his dreams, the sound of a malevolent sea serpent bent on devouring the victims it missed on that hellish day.

"The first blast flung me like a rag doll. There were sirens and screams, 'To the lifeboats. This is not a drill.' I just—" His voice hitched, and as much as he hated breaking down in front of Addy, he'd sunk too deep in the memory to stop now. He shifted his focus to the dark horizon and away from her glistening, sympathetic eyes.

"My mind blanked out most of it. That's a mercy. But I remember the deck swaying under my feet, the flames shooting up like dragon's breath. I remember my heart beating so hard I feared it'd burst right through my chest." He scraped a hand down his sweat-dotted face. "It's a miracle most of us escaped with our lives."

Addy cupped his cheek, her eyes glistening with sympathy. "How many didn't make it?"

"Eleven." Every face, every name was seared in his memory. And he would have been one of them, if not for that hunch.

A low growl came from the wind-twisted cypress where Snoot had been gnawing a rawhide chew. Hackles bristling, growling deep in his throat, he stalked to the bluff's edge.

"What's up, buddy?" Addy started toward her pet, but Kieran yanked her back and clamped his arm tight around her waist.

"She's here."

Chapter Six

♥

Mouth agape, Addy stared at the glowing mist hovering just beyond the bluff's edge. "What is that?" she whispered.

Kieran's strong arm encircled her waist, but his body heat couldn't chase away the chills that raised every tiny hair on her arms and nape. The air seemed to thicken, heavy with static charge, as if lightning were about to strike. But no clouds obscured the full moon's glow—except the mysterious shade floating before them.

"It's the White Widow." Kieran whispered, his breath fanning her cheek.

Icy dread turned her knees to water. When he'd suggested they go out ghost-watching, she'd assumed it was a flirtatious ploy to extend their dinner date. But the spectral form loomed closer and elongated, solidifying into a distinctly human shape.

Kieran's other arm came around her, bracing her against his broad chest. "She's never hurt anyone. She's simply looking for her husband."

Clearer now, a woman with upswept dark hair and trailing white skirts paced back and forth, treading on thin air, a lantern in one hand and a telescope in the other.

"This bluff used to extend further." Kieran's voice was soft but steady. "Over the years, storms wore it away."

As if hearing his words, the specter turned to stare right through them. She was young, her beautiful face contorted in grief, her eyes bottomless dark pools. Her lips moved. "Jonathan?"

The question seemed to come from far away, but the poignancy of that single word brought tears to Addy's eyes, and she shivered in Kieran's arms.

As if addressing a human visitor, Kieran answered, "Just the lighthouse keeper, ma'am."

A faint moan drifted on the wind as the figure turned away to search the horizon again. She gradually faded into mist, and then nothingness.

Tears blurred Addy's vision, her heart heavy with an ache not her own. Or was it? Loss, regret, guilt, trauma—it all swam together in a tide of overwhelming emotion.

"Hey now." Grasping her shoulders, Kieran pulled her into his embrace.

She buried her face against his broad chest. "She never gave up on him."

"No, she never did. They say she died of a broken heart." For the second time that night, he rubbed soothing circles on her back, his gentle touch and reassuring solidity exactly what she needed. Hell, she should be comforting him after the wrenching story he'd just shared.

She wound her arms around his waist and hugged him tight. "What a terrible way to exist, always yearning for what you can never have."

"Hmm." He nuzzled her temple, and his beard tickled pleasantly. "Some say a ghost is a spirit with unfinished business."

Addy chuckled through her tears. "Doesn't that describe everyone?"

Kieran's lips brushed her forehead. "Others say it's merely an echo of strong emotion." He pointed toward a clump of pines near the lighthouse. "She lived where the lighthouse stands now. Grand house, it was. Burned down after she died, and the lighthouse was built on the spot. Perhaps we're just experiencing shadows of the pain she felt here."

"That makes more sense to me." She sighed into the crook of his neck. "I've felt those echoes."

Ghost stories she'd read described lost spirits anchored to a particular place, but her ghosts trailed her everywhere—agonized faces, mangled bodies, ragged voices begging for help.

"I think we've all encountered ghosts. We just rationalize them away." With his fingertip, Kieran lifted her chin until she met his gaze. "Listen, when I invited you up here, I envisioned a cozy evening, not a tsunami of bad memories. I'm sorry if I've caused you pain."

What a cruel twist of fate, meeting someone so compassionate, kind, and enticing when they only had a short time together.

But they had tonight, and the rest of the week. Liv always said that things happen for a reason—and right now, Addy was inclined to agree with her.

She quirked an eyebrow. "Honestly? You had no plans for a post-ghost snuggle?"

Kieran's laugh lines crinkled. "Well, the thought did cross my mind, but the other bits, the flashbacks and painful memories—that's not exactly the cozy date I imagined."

"Yeah, things took an unexpected turn. But such is life, right?" She caressed his cheek, his beard scratchy-soft beneath her palm. "Thank you for trusting me with your story, Kieran the Lighthouse Keeper. You are a brave, wise soul."

His gaze flicked to her lips. "Likewise, Addy the Soldier-Surgeon."

Once again, the air between them thickened, crackling with electricity. But this time, ghosts had nothing to do with it. She rose on tiptoe and tilted her head, a silent invitation.

Eyes dark and glittering, he closed the distance, stopping a millimeter from her lips. "Are you sure?"

"I am."

In her forty-one years, Addy had sampled every flavor of kiss, from dry to slobbery, from clumsy to seductive, but she'd never known a kiss like Kieran's.

A soft caress, a sigh of pleasure, the plushness of his lips contrasting with the gentle scrape of his beard. Pulling back, he held her jaw in his big, callused hands and whispered her name, then sealed his mouth to hers. His heat, his low moans as he teased her lips apart and gently, patiently, learned her mouth with decadent strokes—Kieran's kiss left her breathless, dizzy, completely undone.

After what seemed like hours of swaying together under the moonlight, he broke the kiss and pressed his forehead to hers. "Wow."

"Amen." She giggled, clutching his coat lapels to keep from crumpling to the ground. Every inch of her sizzled with desire.

He relaxed his embrace and rested his hands on her hips. "Addy, love, I know you've got a busy life far away from here, but I'm going to need more of this." He brushed a kiss over her temple. "More of you."

Too lust-drunk to form words, she could only nod. "Yes, please." Steamy visions crowded her brain: Kieran scooping her into his burly arms, carrying her back inside, and tossing her onto his bed before he...

With a rumbling hum of pleasure, he rained kisses over her closed lids, her nose, her cheeks. "There's a helluva Halloween Party at Salty Dog Saloon," he murmured against her temple. "Care to be my date?"

Oops, time to cool her overheated jets before she embarrassed them both. Kieran was a decent, respectful man. Of course he wouldn't rush her into his bed.

"I'd love to. But that's not until Thursday."

And I have to leave a few days after that.

Regret sliced between her ribs.

He nuzzled the sensitive skin behind her ear. "Seems like an eternity, doesn't it? Tomorrow's Sunday, lots of visitors to the lighthouse. Care for a sunset picnic?"

"Mmff." Nodding, she pressed her lips to his. "I'll bring the food."

"No, you're my guest." He licked into her mouth.

Oh, the tantalizing, teasing delight of Kieran's velvet tongue! She had to feel that marvel on her skin, her breasts, between her legs.

She raked her fingers through his short curls, eliciting a sexy grunt from the big man. "Tell you what, why don't you come to my place? I'm renting a cottage on Narwhal Lane. I'll whip up something while you work." She'd wash the sheets, too, just in case.

"If you insist, beauty." He nibbled her lower lip. "But dessert's on me."

Addy whimpered at the mental image of Kieran stretched out naked while she drizzled honey over his body and licked him clean.

What was with her tonight? Must be the shock of seeing the ghost, plus all this messy soul baring that left her feeling completely exposed, nerves sizzling with awareness.

Her usual level-headed caution had gone AWOL. Relinquishing her grip on Kieran's hair, she tunneled her hands beneath his coat, desperate to touch his skin.

But Snoot hadn't got the memo. At the end of his canine patience, her pup chose that moment to press his head between their knees, snuffling and grumbling.

"Sorry, pal." Releasing Addy, Kieran bent to ruffle Snoot's fur. "That's enough monopolizing your mistress for tonight."

Oh, it's not nearly enough.

She sucked in a bracing breath before pecking Kieran's lips. "Thank you, Keeper, for an unforgettable night. I'm looking forward to tomorrow."

"As am I, Doc." He traced her jawline with his forefinger. "Though the memory of kissing you will likely keep me up all night."

Heaven help her, how was she supposed to sleep with the image of Kieran *up* seared into her brain?

Arm in arm, they walked back to the cottage, where Kieran insisted on packing up leftover pie for her to take home.

"All that talking can wear a body out." Eyes gleaming, he pressed the container into her hands. "And you'll need your strength for tomorrow."

Hot damn! Liv was right—this trip to the beach was exactly what she needed.

Chapter Seven

♥

While Addy's poulet basquaise braised in the rental cottage's oven, she stretched out on the squashy sofa, propped her feet on the sea chest coffee table, and opened the journal Liv had assigned her—still mostly empty, except for a few pages devoted to Kieran.

If this sweet little cottage were home, she could take her time figuring out her feelings about him, her next steps, and her pain-in-the-ass family. But "home" was a bland, golf-course condo chosen for its proximity to the base. Funny how this rental made her feel more at home than she ever had in that ultra-modern building.

A line at the top of an empty journal page caught her eye: *The decisions you make are a choice of values that reflect your life in every way. – Alice Waters*

What a weird coincidence, to encounter a quote by a famous chef on the first day in ages she indulged her love of cooking. An eerie tingle danced down Addy's spine.

She tapped her pen on the page. "Okay then, values."

Snoot looked up and thumped his tail on the floor.

"Right you are, my love. I value..."

The dog held her gaze, his liquid brown eyes rapt.

"Time with Snoot." Grinning, she jotted that down. "What else?"

Her buddy heaved a noisy sigh and rested his chin on his crossed forelegs.

"Big help you are." She clicked her pen rapidly for a moment before adding

Service

Duty

Loyalty

"Yeah, but to whom?"

She scribbled *family*, then scratched it out. Then wrote it again.

Since honesty was another of her values, putting family on this list grated like sand in her undies. She chewed on her pen. "Not family per se, but...community? Family of the heart?"

With a snarl of frustration, she scratched through *family* yet again, pressing so hard she tore a hole in the paper.

"Damn it," she growled, then turned the page and printed *SELF CARE* in block letters. After all, Liv insisted she indulge herself on this trip. But what counted as self-care?

Last night had left her feeling very cared for indeed—also seen, heard, even protected. Other than Liv, no one had made her feel that way in ages—not her therapist, and definitely not the hospital's PTSD support group that clammed up as soon as a Lieutenant Colonel entered their circle.

But she couldn't drag Kieran to her next assignment. The sweet, hunky lighthouse keeper had already found his home, and she needed to find hers.

Ironic—cruel, even—how the universe threw a "keeper" like Kieran across her path at a juncture where keeping him was out of the question. If she let herself linger on that thought, she'd get so bogged down in regret she'd be unable to tackle the urgent problems before her.

She nibbled her pen. "I dunno, Snoot. What makes me feel cared for besides hanging out with you?"

The dog sprang up, fetched his tennis ball, and dropped it at her feet.

"Exercise. Good one." She jotted down the word, twisted in her seat, and tossed the ball down the short hallway. Snoot scrabbled after it.

Outdoor time, she added to the list. Didn't get much of that with her long hours in the operating room.

Connection? Friendship?

When the timer dinged, she tucked her journal away and returned to the kitchen, opening drawers until she found a pair of oven mitts shaped like sharks. Cute.

The chicken was almost ready. She popped it back into the oven, planted her hands on her hips, and glanced around. She'd love to live full time in a place like this, colorful and cozy, with plenty of natural light even on an overcast day, and so full of personality. Even the kitchen junk drawer brimmed with tchotchkes that made her smile: a mermaid bottle opener, a lighter shaped like a lighthouse, and a pen printed with a stern sea captain who, when you tilted the pen, shed his pea coat to reveal a buff, bare chest.

Of course, her inner horn-dog pictured Kieran doing the same.

And the refrigerator magnet collection! There must've been one from every business in Trappers Cove. Her favorite was the UFO from Souvenir Galaxy, complete with an alien flashing a peace sign.

A hippie-dippy sun catcher sparkled in the window above the sink, and over the dining table hung an amateurish painting of the castle she'd spotted on a bluff above the north end of the beach. Addy peered closer. Could she do something like this? For years, she'd wanted to try her hand at painting, but her expensive watercolors remained unopened.

When was the last time she'd done something creative, just for the hell of it?

Speaking of creative, she'd need to pull together some kind of Halloween costume for the party Kieran invited her to. She made a mental note to visit that vintage shop on Main Street, the one with flashily dressed mannequins in the window.

She tapped her tablet to check her recipe for Basque-style braised chicken with peppers. She'd fallen in love with this dish, and the picturesque coastal town where she encountered it, on a trip to the South of France before her first deployment. After that sumptuous meal, she walked along the harborside promenade, relishing the soft, salty air. As the sun slipped below the horizon, she'd promised herself that someday she would live by the sea.

A strange, falling sensation yanked her back to the present, as if the ground were shifting under her feet. Heart galloping, Addy gripped the counter. Earthquake?

Her stomach rumbled.

"No, genius, you haven't eaten since breakfast." She cut a slice from the crusty sourdough loaf she bought at Sweet Dreams Bakery, slathered it with butter, and stuffed it into her mouth.

Right on cue, her phone blasted the chorus of ELO's "Evil Woman."

Crap on a cracker, Mom again. If she moved to Nebraska, she'd have to give up the snarky ringtones she'd assigned to her family members: Darth Vader's "Imperial March", Elton John's "The Bitch Is Back," AC/DC's "Highway to Hell."

Screw it—she was here to relax and ponder, not placate and pander, so she let the call go to voicemail and moved to the bathroom to touch up her minimalist makeup—a swipe of mascara, a dusting of blush, and lipstick in a subtle shade of rose.

She was misting on cologne—orange blossom and lemon verbena—when the phone shrilled again. And again.

Well, crap. Perhaps there was a real emergency for once.

"About flippin' time," Betsy Connor squawked in Addy's ear. "I was about to call the base commander."

"You'd never get through to him, Mom." Keeping her voice carefully neutral, Addy flipped her hair upside down and brushed it until it crackled. "What's up?"

"Well," Mom huffed, "this morning, I saw a piece on Wolf News about that PTSD stuff. Terrible! Nightmares, flashbacks, public meltdowns, suicide." Her tone oozed into a saccharine coo. "I'm so worried about you, baby girl. You've served long enough. It's time to come home to your family. Let us take care of you."

Addy barely suppressed a snort. "Mom, I'm forty-one. I handle my business just fine on my own."

"Forty-one? Impossible. I'm too young to have a daughter that old."

Addy dug through her jewelry case and selected a pair of freshwater pearl drop earrings. "Last week, you told me you were too old to manage on your own."

"Don't you get fresh with me, missy," Mom snapped. "You may be a fancy Army officer, but you're still my little girl."

That was the crux of the matter right there—Mom loved babies, but the adults they grew into? Not so much. When Addy became old enough to have ideas of her own, Mom simply made another baby. And another, and another, until the doctor told her the next pregnancy would probably kill her. That's when the "Make me some grandbabies" campaign began.

Addy was the only one of her siblings who hadn't obliged, another black mark on her name.

A sharp bark from Snoot gave her the perfect escape. "Gotta go, Mom. My company's here."

"Company? Who—"

"Talk to you soon." She disconnected and trotted to the front door where Snoot lay flat, tail whipping as if he'd discovered an exciting scent.

Another kiss from Kieran would be the perfect remedy to the bitter taste Mom's call left behind.

"Self-care, self-care, self-care," she whispered as she fluffed her hair and brushed crumbs from her sweater. "And if I'm lucky, one hot night with the sexy ginger keeper."

Chapter Eight

♥

When Addy opened the door, Snoot's enthusiastic greeting nearly knocked Kieran on his ass.

"Snoot, leave it," she commanded, and the Lab subsided, still quivering with excitement.

Addy sucked in a deep breath to keep from wiggling just as hard as her canine buddy, because damn! Kieran looked *good* in an old-fashioned oilskin jacket, dark jeans, and damp boots.

From his backpack, he handed her a plastic cake container and a slightly squashed bouquet of mini sunflowers, orange roses, rust-red mums, and silver-green eucalyptus.

"Sorry. Rain's picked up. Thought I'd enjoy a walk in the mist, but..." Grinning, he removed his jacket and shook it hard, sprinkling the porch with raindrops. He draped it over the bench, then took off his boots before stepping inside.

"Pear and ginger pie this time. Hope that goes well with the delicious dish I'm smelling." He pecked her cheek, treating her to a waft of cologne that smelled like a forest—a secluded grove where she and Kieran could indulge in some naughty, naked fun on a soft bed of pine needles and...

He cleared his throat. "You okay, Addy?" His auburn brows contracted. "You look a little wobbly."

Get your shit together, Connor!

She forced a laugh. "I'm grand. Just forgot to eat lunch. Come in, let's get started."

"Let's start with this." With a hand on the small of her back, he pulled her in for a soft, gentle kiss that quickly deepened to hot, wet bliss.

Addy's knees turned to water.

"Whoa." Kieran chuckled through a wicked grin. "Let's get some food in you before you pass out."

She fetched the platter of apéritif snacks she'd prepared earlier: marinated olives and mushrooms, salted almonds, and fancy crackers.

"I made us a mocktail to start." In truth, she spent far too long this morning diving down an internet rabbit hole before selecting this concoction of ginger beer, honey, lemon, and mint.

When she returned with his glass, she found Kieran setting the table with the dishes and flatware she'd left on the counter, as easy and natural as if they dined together all the time. And he'd rolled up the sleeves on his soft chambray shirt, too. She nearly swooned.

He clinked his glass to hers and sipped. "Wow. Spicy and delicious." The merry twinkle in his eye suggested a deeper meaning. "But really, if you'd prefer something stronger, I don't mind. I just—" He scrubbed his hand through his hair, rumpling it adorably. "When the memories get bad, it's too tempting to drown them, you know? After watching my dad drink away all the best parts of himself, I prefer to avoid alcohol."

"Right." She gently gripped his muscular, ginger-furred forearm. "Thanks for being so open with me, Kieran."

He lifted a shoulder. "Why not? You and I have a lot in common. Might as well enjoy this connection while it lasts."

A flicker of sadness passed over his gaze, almost too quick to notice, then disappeared. "So." He stabbed a mushroom with a souvenir cocktail fork. "Are you any closer to choosing your path?"

"Perhaps a little. Like you said last night—gotta list the pros and cons, then give it all time to marinate." Chasing a slippery olive with her fork, she confessed, "I'm not the best at making quick decisions. Not big ones that matter, anyway."

"I'm the other way 'round." He speared an olive with impressive dexterity. "I listen to my gut." He nudged her knee with his. "Probably should use my head more often, eh?"

That twinkle in his eye made her feel like the two of them were conspiring to do something delightfully naughty instead of just sharing salty snacks. She nudged him back. "Seems to me you're doing well. You've found a job that fits your storyteller's soul and a home with a view to die for."

"That I have." He gave a lopsided grin. "And until recently, I was content living there alone."

Sparks danced along her nerves like Morse code. "How recently?"

His fingertips brushed the back of her hand. "Quite recently."

Holy smoke, this flirtation was heating up fast. Belly quivering with excitement, Addy scurried to the kitchen to fetch their dinner. She set the Dutch oven on a trivet—shaped like a pair of orcas, of course.

Kieran took a big sniff of the fragrant steam and moaned.

A zing of awareness sizzled over Addy's skin, settling at the apex of her thighs. Kieran Gallagher was going to be the death of her. Or maybe her rebirth?

Slamming a lid onto that dangerous thought, she served him a big scoop of rice pilaf and topped it with golden chicken, meltingly soft red and green peppers, and crimson sauce. "Basque-style chicken. I hope you like it."

He took a bite, chewed for a moment, then clapped a hand to his heart and slumped back in his seat as if he'd been shot. "Incredible."

"Pfft." Secretly delighted, she waved off the compliment with a flick of her fingers. "It's just stewed chicken."

"What's the spice?" He forked up another big bite.

"The recipe calls for piment d'Espelète, which is hard to find, but I found Aleppo pepper at the Food Co-op. Not bad for a small-town grocery store."

He gave her a crooked grin. "We're not completely unciv-ilized here. The Co-op even offers gourmet cooking lessons the first Saturday of the month. Maybe you could come down next month?"

She clenched her napkin. "Oh, I..."

Kieran's smile slipped a little. "Of course, you must be very busy."

Well, crap. Way to spoil the mood.

She laid her hand over his. "Look, Kieran, I like you and I like this place. I hope to come back soon, but I'm not in a position to make any promises."

"Of course. I understand." He gave her hand a gentle squeeze. "Tell you what—tomorrow's my day off. What do you say to a tour of the town?" He waggled his eyebrows. "I know all the best places."

She laughed and dug into her own portion. "All right, you're on."

Kieran mopped up a smear of sauce with his bread. "I hope last night's visit from the White Widow didn't trouble your sleep."

"Oh, I didn't dream of the ghost." Not the one they saw last night, anyway. Her dreams had been a swirl of wrenching memories: overcrowded hospital bays, blood-smeared hands clutching at her scrubs, ragged voices pleading for relief from the pain. And there at the end of the endless corridor stood Kieran, dressed like an orderly and asking, "How can I help?"

Her frantic dream-self shoved medical implements into his hands—syringes and IV bags and scalpels—barking orders until he stumbled backward and dropped the lot, slicing a long gash on his leg.

"Great," she'd cried, "now I'll have to stitch you up too."

But Kieran wasn't flustered tonight. Leaning onto his elbows, holding her gaze, he looked ready to take on all her baggage.

Wishful thinking, much? She gave her head a little shake. "Sorry, wandered off for a moment."

"Happens to the best of us." Reaching across the table, he took both her hands in his. "Ready for some pie?"

Arousal crackled along her nerves, but he only meant dessert, damn it. She pulled herself together and rose to clear away the plates, but Kieran beat her to it. "You cook, I clean."

She trailed him into the kitchen. "But you did both jobs last night."

He threw a playful glance over his shoulder. "Are you always this contentious?"

He set the dishes in the sink, then clasped her shoulders, brushed a soft kiss over her lips, and steered her back to her seat. "You have so much responsibility in your life, but right now, you're on vacation. Let someone else take charge for a moment."

Hoo boy, did she want to let Kieran take charge! What would it be like to place herself in his strong, work-roughened hands? To feel his skin against hers, his beard tickling her breasts, his hot, wicked mouth gliding down, down, down—

His powerful thigh brushed her arm as he set down a plate with a large slice of streusel-topped pie.

Flushing hotly, she stared from the dessert to his face. He rotated his chair, straddled it, sturdy thighs spread wide, and forked up a big bite. "This is a new recipe. I want to know what you think, Addy." He raised the morsel to her mouth.

Her lips closed around flakey crust, plump fruit, and sweet spice. A moan of bliss escaped before she could rein it in.

Kieran's gaze lasered onto her lips. His voice rumbled like distant thunder—not yet dangerous, but closing fast. "There's nothing sexier than a beautiful woman surrendering to pleasure."

Heat coursed through her veins, frying her last thread of restraint. Driven by something more powerful than common sense, she shoved the plate aside, fisted his shirt, and tugged him into a devouring kiss.

Kieran's mouth was a wonder of silken heat. Spearing his fingers into her hair, he took control, angling her head to stroke deeper, melting away all thoughts of ticking clocks and consequences.

A low growl and a nudge on her calf reminded her they weren't alone.

Chuckling, Kieran broke the kiss. "Hey, buddy, I'm not hurting her." His gaze softened as he cupped Addy's cheek. "I'd never do that."

Addy blew out a breath and arranged her features in a semblance of calm. "Kieran's our friend, Snoot."

Head tilted, the dog looked from her face to Kieran's, trying to decode this new behavior. And that's when it hit her—in the year plus that Snoot had been her companion, he'd never seen her kissing a man. Not until yesterday.

She ruffled his furry head. "All good, love. Now, bed." She pointed to the cushion near the hearth.

With a canine grumble, Snoot slunk to his bed, circled, and lay down.

Kieran grasped Addy's hand and dropped soft kisses over her knuckles. "Perhaps we should take this to another room?" His eyebrows flicked up, and oh—those dancing hazel eyes, sparkling with mischief. He scanned her body, and...

Oh God, I'm going to get naked with this man!

She braced herself for an icy wash of insecurity, her usual reaction to undressing with a new partner, but the feeling never came, dispelled by the hunger in Kieran's gaze. He wanted this as much as she did.

A wicked grin stretched her lips. Liv prescribed self-care this week, and Addy had a hunch that Kieran was going to care for her needs until her bones melted.

Chapter Nine

♥

Kieran fought for control, but kissing Addy shut down his rational mind, leaving a ravening animal inside the skin that once housed a careful, sensible man—before he met the beautiful doctor and remembered what it was to crave not just a woman's touch, but her tenderness, her companionship, her...

Love?

That inner whisper echoed, revving his pulse even higher than Addy's kiss did.

He'd heard stories about love at first sight and all that malarkey. Blame it on the hormones, or loneliness, or too much time away from his therapy group, but right now, Kieran wanted a hell of a lot more than sex with Addy. There was something magical about her, a rare honesty and openness he hadn't known he needed until she arrived on his doorstep.

Searching his eyes, Addy threaded her fingers into his hair. Her smile dazzled like sunlight on the water as she took his hand and backed toward the hallway. "Shall we?"

Heat curled up his spine. Too bewitched to speak, he followed.

When they reached the closed bedroom door, she leaned against it, her breasts rising on a deep inhalation.

Kieran held his breath. *Please, Addy, don't change your mind. We both need this.*

The sexy way she bit her lip had him hard as iron. He needed to drink in every inch of her, to touch and taste and claim.

But she wasn't his. A week from tonight, he'd watch her taillights disappear from Trappers Cove.

Still, the military base was only three hours away, and although they'd only shared a few kisses, he was dead certain one night with Addy Connor would never be enough.

"Come on, slowpoke." She interrupted his strategizing with a kiss hot enough to burn his clothes right off his body. She pulled back and gazed up at him, her brow rumpled in worry. "Or are you having second thoughts?"

He pressed his palms to the door, caging her in. "No, darlin'. Just pondering how to make this so good, you'll come back for more."

A flicker of darkness passed over her face, quickly replaced by a devilish smile. "That's a tall order. Think you're up for the challenge?"

Beautiful, kind, and snarky too? This woman absolutely slayed him.

"Listen, Addy." He pressed his body to hers from chest to hips, letting her feel the hard ridge of his arousal. "Up is an insufficient word for the state you've got me in." He traced the shell of her ear with the tip of his tongue, then kissed the silky skin beneath. "And I love a challenge."

She shivered, and damn if her response didn't flood his veins with fire. This woman would be his undoing. Fisting her hair at her nape, he took her mouth in a kiss so frantic their teeth clashed.

Her soft whimper set his heart thrashing behind his ribs. He clutched her luscious ass and lifted her off her feet. Just as starved for pleasure as he was, she clasped her thighs around his hips, gasping when her center lined up with his aching erection, and *Gods above!*—she rocked her pelvis, nearly bringing him off in his trousers like a lust-mad kid.

"Kieran, I need—" She cut off her plea with another searing kiss, her pie-sweet tongue delving into his mouth.

Still holding her aloft, he flung the door open and lurched toward the bed. Everything in him demanded he strip off both their clothes, sink into her softness, and race to the climax they both craved, but if he had a hope of earning more than one unforgettable night with Addy, he had to show her what she'd be missing when she left.

When they collided with the mattress, he dipped his knees and gently set her down. Holy angels, the look she gave him as she reclined on her back, arms above her head, her hair spread out on the pillow, her glistening lips parted—pure desire and sweet promise.

Now that she lay before him, welcoming him into her bed, all his words deserted him except "Beautiful Addy." Raining kisses over her face and neck, he slid his hands beneath her sweater. Her skin was a satiny miracle, warm and giving, and her breasts! Cloud-soft, full and heavy, they filled his hands perfectly. He had to taste them.

"Can I take this off?" He tugged at their lace cage.

"If you'll take your shirt off first." Eyes glittering, she pulled his shirttails free from his belt. "I want to see you, Kieran."

And just like that, anxiety stomped on the brakes. Taking off his shirt meant baring his scars, and previous lovers had quailed at the shiny, puckered slashes across his back, spoiling the mood with their squeamishness, pity, and questions. If Addy flinched—

She's a doctor, he reminded himself. *She's seen worse.*

Straddling her, he leaned down and traced the delicate line of her jaw with his forefinger. "Addy, I was burned in the rig fire."

She nodded slowly. "I've seen lots of burns, Kieran. And the aftermath, for those lucky enough to survive."

Damn it—now who was spoiling the mood?

She reached up and cupped his cheek in her soft palm. "I promise you, no amount of scarring will make me want you less."

Heart thundering, he watched her slender fingers release the front clasp on her bra. Her glorious breasts spilled out, ripe and inviting.

He reached for them, but she grasped his wrists firmly. "Shirt off."

"Bossy, aren't you?" Grinning to cover his fear, he unfastened his buttons and tugged the garment over his head.

With a cock-firing mewl, Addy ran her hands over his furry front as if memorizing the planes and angles of him.

"You're beautiful," she whispered and clasped the back of his neck, drawing him down into a deep, searching kiss. Chest to chest, belly to belly, they undulated until he couldn't endure one second more.

Rearing up, he pinned her wrists above her head. "Here's what's going to happen, love." He reached for the waistband of her jeans. "I'm going to peel this off you, set my poor langer free before it catches fire, and then..." He trailed kisses down her pale throat and over her collar bones before latching onto one puckered, rosy nipple. Addy gasped and bucked beneath him.

"And then?"

He circled her other taut bud with his tongue. "And then, my beautiful doc, I'm going to give you a hundred reasons to return to me."

Head lolling, she closed her eyes and arched her back.

True to his word, he sloooowly slid her jeans over her smooth legs, kissing and nipping each revealed inch of tender skin. He tongued the backs of her knees, the hollows behind her ankle bones, before rising again until he reached the silky skin of her inner thighs, just below her lace knickers.

Red, he noted. She'd been planning this encounter, and the thought of this woman dressing for him, brushing her dark-chocolate hair until it gleamed, dabbing that spring-fresh scent between her breasts and in the hollow of her throat as she fantasized...

"Addy," he moaned and kissed her mound through the cloth, then hooked his fingers through the elastic and whisked away the last barrier between her flesh and his hungry mouth.

And oh, the wonder of her, plush and glistening with arousal! He gave her seam one long lick, drawing a gasp from her kiss-stung lips.

"That's my girl," he growled and gripped her thighs, forcing them farther apart. "Let me see you, all seashell pink and wet for me."

She writhed, canting her hips up in a silent plea for more.

"Like that, do you?" He indulged her with a flurry of licks and flicks and deep, sucking kisses. His Addy wasn't one to keep still—in fact, her wriggling dance brought her to the edge of the mattress with one toned leg dangling.

"Easy now." Rising to his knees, he grasped her hips and tugged her back to the center of the bed. He cast his gaze on the brass headboard. "Maybe I should tie you up to keep you from falling out of bed."

Addy's eyes widened, and—bless her randy heart—she reached above her head and grasped the brass railing.

"Good girl." Closing his fingers over her slender wrists, he covered her nude body with his half-clothed one and ground his throbbing cock between her splayed thighs.

"Ouch," she complained. "Your belt buckle."

"You want me naked, beauty?"

"Desperately." Wanton need flickered in her jade irises.

Never had he felt more desired. A feral grin curled his lips as he released her and stripped off his jeans, undershorts, and then bent to remove his socks—because there's nothing more ridiculous than a man wearing nothing but a stiff cock and his socks.

In doing so, he exposed his back to her. The mattress creaked, and soft fingers stroked his ragged skin. He braced himself for her reaction, but no words came, only a gentle kiss between his shoulder blades.

That sweet gesture melted something deep inside him, a defensive wall he hadn't lowered for anyone since the disaster. Tears prickled his eyes. Blinking them back, he rounded on her and pressed her into the mattress.

"Sweet Addy." He slid his hand between their bodies and parted her folds, plunging his middle finger into her liquid heat while his palm cupped her mound. Massaging gently, he probed with his thumb until he found the firm bud of her clit. He licked into her mouth, stroking her in time with his movements below.

Addy moaned and jerked, her stomach muscles clenched, her legs tight around his hips. He thrust another finger inside her, pumping slowly, all the while angling his cock away to keep from spilling himself on her thigh. Head flung back, she squeezed her eyes shut and keened, her inner walls gripping his fingers.

"That's it, love. Let go. I've got you." Clutching her tight, he kissed her arched throat as she rode out the throes of her climax.

With a sharp tug on his hair and a sexy growl, Addy threw her thigh over him and rolled him onto his back, rising above him on hands and knees. Eyes glittering, she grasped his cock and notched it at her entrance. Every instinct demanded he plunge into her slick heat, but he gritted out a strangled, "Condom!"

"Right." With a laugh, Addy swiped her snarled hair out of her eyes and dove toward the nightstand.

Kieran beat her to it, his fingers closing around a foil packet.

"Ready for tonight, were ya?"

"Hopeful." She bit her lip, and her gaze lasered onto his cock as he quickly sheathed himself and clutched her flushed, sweat-slicked body to his.

"How do you want me, love?"

"Every way." Her teeth closed on the flesh of his shoulder, a bright flash of pain that fired his blood even hotter.

He rolled atop her and pinned her hands above her head, reveling in her needy whimpers. Holding her gaze, he sank into the heaven between her thighs—liquid heat that hugged him tight and filled his mind with stars.

"Addy, you're so..." He couldn't finish the thought because she seized his mouth in a greedy kiss.

He did his best to rein in his driving need, but when she arched her back and screamed his name, his control shattered. Bucking like a wild beast, he rammed into her again and again, her cries of pleasure ringing in his ears as his own climax roared through him.

Afterward, when his vision cleared and his breath slowed enough for speech, he gathered Addy into his arms and breathed in the springtime fragrance of her bed-mussed hair. What could he possibly say to her? Words were not adequate to the task of describing how *changed* he felt—at once relaxed and uplifted and transformed and feckin' marvelous, and all of it thanks to this beautiful, generous woman who saw his wounds up close and still welcomed him into her bed, her mind, her glorious body.

And now, the only question pulsing through him: how to win her heart?

Chapter Ten

♥

That was...

Addy lay on her side and traced swirls on Kieran's skin, her body thrumming with the impact of the most devastating, delicious, divine sex of her life. How had she made it to age forty-one and never known lovemaking could be this good? Drunk on pleasure, her analytical brain struggled to comprehend what had just happened between her and Kieran.

Quit overthinking, she scolded herself. *Don't spoil this fleeting moment.*

But the process had already begun, ephemeral joy fading into cold reality. Giving herself to this amazing man, joining their bodies in bliss, talking and laughing into the night...none of that solved anything on her to-do list of impossible decisions.

But oh, the pleasure of his feather-light touch as he traced her silhouette from shoulder to hip in a slow, lingering exploration. Kieran Gallagher was a master of afterglow.

His soft lips pressed to her forehead. "Happy, love?"

Love. He'd called her that several times now—probably just a linguistic quirk from his Irish roots, right? Nothing to get worked up about or build her hopes on.

"I am," she answered truthfully, returning his kiss. "You, Kieran Gallagher, are a talented man."

A sheen of pink tinged his cheeks. "I'm an inspired man, thanks to you." His warm hazel eyes glowed in the low light of her bedside lamp. "I've never felt this good, Addy, not with anyone." He raked his fingers into her hair, and the soft scratch of his callused fingertips on her scalp coaxed a whimper from her throat. "Promise me this wasn't our only night."

"I promise." Though the clock was ticking toward her departure from Trappers Cove, while she was here, Addy could no more deny this man his place in her bed than she could deny her next breath.

"So tell me." She rubbed her calf over his hairy, muscular one. "What are you wearing to the Halloween party?"

His chuckle rumbled through his chest, tickling her bare breasts. "My lady is hiding behind small talk."

His lady. She liked the sound of that entirely too much. And his understanding of her inner workings was entirely too sharp.

Forcing a carefree smile, she spiraled her fingertip through the russet thatch on his chest. "How can I hide when I'm naked?"

Chuckling, he kissed the top of her head. "It's all right. I feel it too, beauty. Tonight rattled my bones good and proper."

His smile slipped a little as his gaze probed hers. "Make no mistake, Doctor Addy, I aim to keep you. And I'm a patient man."

What the hell was she supposed to say to a declaration like that?

Kieran released and rolled onto his back, cradling his head in his hands, which caused his biceps to bunch distractingly. "Be that as it may, my Halloween costume is top secret."

"Uh huh." She nestled her cheek into the perfect hollow between his pec and shoulder. "I'll bet you have no idea what you're wearing."

"No, I don't." His laugh shook them both.

"Well, if we're going to the party together, shouldn't we match?"

He nuzzled her hair and kissed her forehead. "I rather like the way we don't match. And yet, we fit, you know? Like contrasting flavors that make a dish more delicious. Speaking of..." He rolled up and bounded out of bed. "I promised you pie, didn't I? How about dessert in bed?"

Giggling, Addy surveyed the room—clothing strewn over floor and furniture, covers torn off the bed. "We've already made a mess of the place. What's a few crumbs?"

"I like the way you think, Doc." Kieran cocked a finger pistol at her as, splendidly naked, he backed toward the door, his half-erect cock bobbing.

"I like you too, Keeper." Smiling so hard her cheeks burned, she flopped back onto the pillows.

After she and Kieran decimated multiple slices of pie and shook the crumbs from the sheets, he hugged her tight, kissed the top of her head, and sighed. The cottage lay silent except for rain thrumming on the roof.

"I should probably head out," he murmured into her hair.

All this talk of keeping her, and he didn't want to spend the night? Disappointment needled her. "Is that what you want, Kieran?"

"To leave you alone?" His chuckle was tinged with chagrin. "Not at all."

As if the gods had scripted it, a thunderclap rumbled, tightening Addy's skin into goosebumps.

Kieran pulled back and studied her. "Scared of thunder?"

She shook her head. "I know it's not mortar fire, but tell that to my jumpy nerves."

He nibbled his lip a moment, a project she'd gladly help him with, then his tense expression relaxed into a soft smile. "Then I'll stay."

"Good." Looping her arms around his nape, she kissed him, sipping at his lips, chasing sweetness from the pie combined with the unique, comforting taste of Kieran himself.

He's right, she thought, nestling into his strong arms. *We're so different, but we fit.*

Humming low to drown out the thunder, Kieran held her close. A last thought drifted through her before surrendering to sleep:

This is perfect.

A shout and a shove jerked Addy from her cozy dream. Clutching the sheet to her bare chest, she bolted from the bed and glanced wildly around, searching for cover.

"Lifeboats!" Kieran screamed, his arms and legs thrashing, his eyes squinched shut.

Addy's heart hammered her ribs. She'd read about PTSD-induced night terrors, and her own nightmares sometimes jerked her awake, yet Kieran appeared to be deep asleep, unaware of her presence. He was a big man, outweighing her by a good sixty pounds. How to help him without injuring him or herself?

She edged around the mattress, moving closer to the door in case she needed to escape. "Kieran?"

"Run!" he bellowed and rolled onto his side, legs pinwheeling as he sprinted through his nightmare.

"Kieran, honey, you're okay. You're safe," she crooned and gently touched his shoulder.

He seized her hand and clung tight. "Mmmfffah." He was slowing now, his panicked cries fading into incoherence, his movements sluggish.

"Easy, I've got you." She slid into bed beside him.

With a soft moan, he curled his big body around her as shudders ran through him.

Her heart squeezed like a fist at the sight of him, trapped in a replay of the worst day of his life. Softly, she stroked his rigid shoulder. "It's okay, love. You're not alone."

His breathing evened out, and bit by bit, his body went soft and heavy with sleep, his arm draped across her middle as she stared into the night.

"Oh, Kieran, look at us," she whispered. "Two wounded souls who crashed together."

Had tonight's intensity ricocheted him back to a dark place? And could she help him out of it?

Not likely, burdened as she was with her own heavy baggage.

As if hearing her thoughts, Kieran shifted and laid his head over her heart, washing her in a wave of tenderness that stung her eyes with tears. She couldn't resist stroking his soft curls.

"Wha...Addy?" He pushed up on one arm and peered at her, bleary-eyed. "Can't sleep?"

"No, I uh..." She hesitated a moment, then decided honesty was the kindest, most respectful approach. "You had a nightmare."

He bolted upright and whisked the sheet down, his gaze raking her bare skin. "Did I hurt you?"

She raised her palms in a placating gesture. "No, no, not at all. Scared me pretty good, though." She gave a weak laugh. "You seemed to be running for your life."

Kieran dragged his hand down his face. "Shite on a stick." He softly clasped her arms. "Addy, I am so sorry. It's been a long time since I had an episode like that. I thought I'd moved past it." His broad shoulders slumped. "Talk about bad timing."

"Hey now." She wound her arm around his waist. "We both have our battle scars. I don't know anyone who's reached our age without at least a few."

The look he gave her was solemn. "I could've hurt you, Addy. I'd better go."

Before she could protest, he pushed to his feet and collected his clothes.

"Wait, didn't you walk here?"

He moved to the window and peered into the darkness. "Rain's stopped. The fresh air will clear my head." He made for the door.

"Kieran!" She stepped across his path and planted her hand on his chest. "What we shared tonight—it meant something to me. Don't shut me out."

He raised her hand to his lips. "It meant something to me as well, Addy." His expression softened. "This isn't goodbye. I just need a bit of space, that's all." He kissed her palm, a sweet gesture that stole her breath.

And so, wrapped up in a blanket, she stood in the doorway of her rental cottage and watched Kieran stride into the darkness.

Chapter Eleven

♥

Wrapped in a blanket that still held Kieran's woodsy scent, Addy dragged herself into the kitchen, filled the teakettle, and stared out the window at drizzly rain dripping from glossy madrona leaves. She should be sharing this peaceful moment with her new friend, but he'd bolted into the night.

Her heart ached for him, and for herself. Other than Liv, it had been ages since she'd met anyone so easy to talk to. Kieran's warm, steady gaze held so much promise—but now, his absence echoed in the once-cozy cottage.

Damn it to hell and back, this was so unfair! First, her own PTSD threatened the military career she'd called home for eleven years. And now that she'd finally met a man who really *got* her, who busted through her defensive walls and gave her supernova orgasms, echoes of his own trauma menaced their budding connection.

How could she persuade Kieran to trust her with his darkness?

She filled a mug with steaming water, dunked in a tea bag, and trudged to the sofa. Snoot hopped up beside her and rested his chin on her thigh, his liquid eyes brimming with concern.

"I know, Bud." She stroked his sleek head. "I miss him too, but he needs space." She slumped against the cushions.

"Which usually means the guy has changed his mind." She sipped the tea, scalding her tongue, then set the mug down too hard and sloshed scorching liquid over her knuckles.

"Crap on a cracker!" She blew on the injured skin, which didn't do a damn thing to ease the sting. Neither did Snoot's tongue-swipe.

Tears prickled Addy's eyes, and she hugged the Lab tightly. He rested his head on her shoulder and sighed.

"I've had one-night stands before, you know? Sometimes it was my idea, and sometimes the guy was dishonest about what he wanted, but Kieran seemed so sincere. And a guy who's just out to get laid says all his sweet words before sex, not after."

Snoot woofed softly.

"You're right. I'll text him."

The dog nudged her cheek with his cold nose.

"Just once, then I'll let him be."

She fetched her phone from its charging stand and tapped out,

> Last night was amazing. Please don't let one bad dream come between us. When you're ready to talk, I'm here.

After a trot on the beach with Snoot, Addy checked her phone again. Still no response from Kieran, who'd promised her a tour of the town and some special spot on the beach today before...

"Well, he's not here, is he?" Addy forced a grim smile as she brushed out her wind-tangled hair. "And I'm not going to waste a beautiful day waiting for a call that might never come."

She left Snoot with a new bully stick and headed into town, disappointment weighing her steps. "Fake it till you feel it," she muttered, but when she rounded the corner onto Main Street, the kitschy Halloween decorations coaxed a genuine smile to her lips. Even in the off season, Trappers Cove embraced the funky, joyfully tacky vibe that drew tourists all summer. So much more fun than her bland, new-construction neighborhood near the base.

She started with the little shops of Souvenir Galaxy, an UFO-themed outdoor mini mall where tinsel spiders, bats, and witches on broomsticks dangled over the brick pathways. The window displays were cute, colorful, and inviting, but nothing tempted her inside to buy. If Liv were here, she'd probably leave with armloads of shopping bags, but shopping alone? Meh.

Next door, the sugary, yeasty smells drifting from Sweet Dreams Bakery reminded her she'd skipped breakfast. Fortified with an almond Danish and an Earl Gray tea, she packed her sourdough loaf into her canvas tote and continued up Main Street, passing art galleries,—*Why decorate when I'm moving soon?*, a neon-lit arcade—*Kid stuff,* and the cute bookstore—*Already been there.*

Pretty pathetic how, in a beach town brimming with amusements, nothing tempted her to play, or sample, or indulge. Kieran's rejection had morphed her into a world-class grump.

Across the street, a garish window display caught her eye.

"Madame Zora's Psychic Emporium." She chuckled. "Well, that's different."

She moved closer to inspect the life-size skeleton wearing a tie-dyed T-shirt and holding a wicked-looking carved dagger. Real jack-o'-lanterns spilled glittering crystals from their grinning mouths. LED candles flickered from brass candelabras draped with spider webs, and a menagerie of figurines—dragons, elves, fairies, trolls, Sasquatch, space aliens—danced around the tableau's centerpiece, a glowing crystal skull.

"Very creative," Addy murmured and stepped through the door.

The doorway bell's merry tinkle greeted her, along with soothing pan flute music. And wow, what a riot of colors and scents! A stone Buddha on the counter wafted patchouli-rose incense. Racks of rainbow-hued clothing crowded the narrow aisle, bumping up against book racks, glass display cases, trickling mini-fountains, hanging macrame plant holders, musical instruments from faraway lands, and an alluring array of crystals, some raw, others carved into pillars, wands, angels, skulls, dragons...

The proprietor, a short, round, grandmotherly woman with a pouf of gray curls and enormous dangly earrings, was busy at the counter helping a customer, so Addy drifted to the crystal display, running her fingers over their smooth coolness, their jagged points. So many colors and textures. Fascinating, to think of all these beauties hiding in the earth.

A touch on her arm made her jump.

With a squeak, Addy set down the crystal she was examining and clapped her palm over her heart. "Sorry, you startled me."

The old hippie mama smiled up at Addy, her dark eyes twinkling. "Jumpy, aren't you?" She gave Addy's arm a comforting pat. "I'm Zora. Tell me, what's troubling you, dear?"

Hard to imagine a less frightening personage than this sweet-faced woman, dressed in Birkenstocks, leggings, and a fluttery batik tunic. Something about her smile invited trust.

"Too many things to count," Addy confessed. "But mostly, I'm stuck on how to help a friend."

"Ah?" Zora lifted a questioning eyebrow.

She was sorely tempted to pour it all out to this sympathetic stranger, but—

"It's not really my place to explain his troubles."

"I see." Zora nodded sagely. "You're a good friend for keeping his secrets." She tilted her head toward a carved wooden screen at the back of the shop. "Tell you what—I know a way to offer insight without divulging sensitive information. Are you willing to try?"

What would that involve, Addy wondered? Crystal balls? Palmistry?

"On the house," Zora added with a wink.

Addy shrugged. "Okay. Why not?"

"Excellent!" Zora beamed and rubbed her palms together. "But first, let's find the stone you need. Hmm..." She ran a fingertip along the shelves. "What's your favorite color?"

"Green."

"And when's your birthday?"

What did that have to do with pretty rocks? "June twenty-sixth."

The little hippie mama nodded sagely. "Cancer. A homebody and a natural caretaker."

A less polite person would've snorted in the old gal's face. Ever since she left Smithsville, Addy took military life's frequent moves in stride, and she damn sure wasn't feeling very nurturing towards her family.

If Zora sensed her skepticism, she didn't let on. "Cancer is a cardinal water sign," she continued, examining another basket of stones. "You're like a flowing river, always moving, navigating around difficulties and other people. Cancers require healing rest because they give so much and care so deeply. Ah!" She lifted a basket full of polished stones striped with shades of green from brightest emerald to darkest pine. "Malachite is excellent for centering your psyche and making decisions when you're in a state of emotional distress."

"Sounds perfect." She couldn't care less about that zodiac nonsense, but the stones were beautiful, reminding her of the deep-green Pacific Northwest forests she'd soon leave behind. She sifted them through her fingers, enjoying their cool heft, and finally selected a heart-shaped pendant.

"Good choice," Zora remarked. "Wear it over your heart to guide you as you tackle whatever's got you so on edge. Now, come with me."

Addy followed her behind the screen to find the quintessential fortuneteller's lair: a table draped in purple velvet, holding a by-God crystal ball and flanked by two plush armchairs. An antique sideboard held an ornate silver samovar and china teacups.

"Here, you'll find this relaxing." Zora filled a delicate cup with fragrant, spicy tea. "My special blend. Have a seat."

She sat opposite Addy, removed the crystal ball, and winked. "That's for the tourists. Locals get the real deal." She interlaced her fingers and cracked her knuckles, then pulled out a deck of tarot cards wrapped in red silk.

Addy's skepticism must've bled through her smile, because Zora added, "Just one card, dear. What can it hurt?"

Chiding herself for the shiver that raised goosebumps on her arms, Addy shrugged. "I guess forward progress requires a leap of faith, right?"

"It does indeed. Now, concentrate on the question you most need answered in this moment."

That was easy. *What the hell is my next step?*

"Got it."

While Zora shuffled, cards sliding through her hands like water, Addy wondered what Liv would say if she were here. Hell, she'd probably laugh and ask for a reading—tarot cards, palmistry, crystal ball, the works. Though a woman of science, Liv had a taste for adventure and a sense of humor—qualities Addy could use more of at this juncture.

Zora fanned the deck face-down on the table. "Pick the card that calls to you."

Really, none of them did, so Addy picked one at random. Zora turned it over.

"Ah." She nodded. "A very profound card."

Addy peered at the illustration. This could not bode well—naked men, women, and children rising out of coffins, their arms raised toward an angel blowing a trumpet.

"Judgment," Zora intoned, confirming Addy's fears. "This card heralds absolution and the completion of a significant undertaking. It symbolizes learning from past life experiences, leading to a spiritual awakening." She tapped the card with her forefinger. "Does that ring true?"

"I suppose. I'm in a place where I have to choose a path, but..." She snarled her fingers into her hair. "How do I decide? And why are these people naked?"

"Nudity symbolizes vulnerability and self-forgiveness."

"Huh." What did she need to forgive in herself? Surviving where others didn't? Giving up on her toxic family? Both goals made perfect sense in her head, but in her guilt-addled gut, those battles were far from over.

"Life-altering decisions require lots of self-reflection," Zora said. "To achieve personal growth, you've gotta peer under heavy rocks and examine all the ugly, squiggly things hiding there." The older woman's grin was infectious.

"Yeah, I've definitely got some ugly squigglies."

Zora patted her hand. "We all do, dear. Don't hide from them. You know what they say about bugs—they're more afraid of you than you are of them." She gave Addy's hand a squeeze. "Just be honest with yourself and listen to your intuition." She tapped the card again. "And there's good news."

"Oh?"

"The card is upright, which suggests you're about to recognize your true intention. You're standing on a promontory, overlooking all you've done and learned. Use this new perspective to heal your psychic wounds and move forward from the past."

New perspective? Well, she was in a new place, meeting new people. Perhaps this time away from the hurry and pressure of her workaday life would reveal some crucial detail she'd missed.

"Okay, um, thanks very much," she said, her voice a little shaky. "You've given me a lot to think about."

"That's my job, dear heart. I open people's eyes to fresh viewpoints."

The doorway bell tinkled, signaling a customer's arrival, and Zora pushed her seat back. "Excuse me, Doctor. Come up when you're ready."

Addy's brows slammed together. "How did you know?"

Grinning, Zora tapped the inside of Addy's wrist.

"Oh, right." A self-conscious flush heated Addy's cheeks as she touched the tiny caduceus tattoo, souvenir of a drunken night out with her fellow first-year residents.

The old gal probably had no more psychic powers than Snoot did, but she was a keen observer, and her woo-woo advice was worth considering.

At the counter, Addy asked, "By the way, that tea is delicious. Do you sell it?"

"Good, isn't it?" Zora pointed to a wire display rack. "This blend comes from Del Toro Botanicals, right here in Trappers Cove. Organic sage, blackberry leaves, lemon verbena, and ginger. Excellent remedy for overthinking."

Addy paid for her purchases and, wandering home in a bit of a daze, contemplated the eerie tarot card, at once creepy and yet kind of...hopeful?

"Holy crud!" she exclaimed as she reached the cottage. "I wanted to ask her how to help Kieran." Perhaps Zora's message held something useful on that matter as well.

She chewed on that question as she unpacked her purchases and assembled a monstrous sandwich, truly a work of culinary art, but when she lifted it to her lips, her stomach twisted.

"Well, shit." She set it on the counter with a disgusted sigh.

Attentive at her feet, Snoot wagged his tail, hoping she'd drop him some scraps.

"Sorry, Bud. Can't have you getting an upset tummy in a rental."

She checked her phone. Still no response from Kieran.

Her mind spinning, she stared at the sandwich. And stared. And stared.

"Well, why not?" she asked Snoot. "We connected over food twice now. Maybe…"

Humming to herself, she assembled another sandwich, washed two apples, and brewed a thermos of Zora's tea, then tucked the picnic into her backpack.

Snoot needed his midday walk anyway, and some brisk exercise in the salty air would revive her appetite. She picked up the leash. "Come on, boy. Let's go visit the keeper."

Chapter Twelve

♥

"Well, shite." Kieran sank onto a sea-smoothed log and stared out at the whispering surf, steady and gentle...and totally indifferent to his aching heart. Cruelly ironic that his day off had dawned bright and mild, perfect weather for convincing Addy to make Trappers Cove her new home.

But no, he'd let a nightmare rattle him and fled her cozy bed, her soft, willing body, her compassionate smile.

"I'm a bleedin' eejit." He plucked a smooth stone from the sand and tossed it toward the foam. Mistaking it for food, a seagull fluttered after it, then flapped back to land at Kieran's feet.

"It'd serve me right if she never talked to me again."

The bird ruffled its feathers and stared at him with bright, beady eyes.

"Probably thinks I used her for my own selfish pleasure. That's what I'd assume in her shoes." He pulled a half-eaten granola bar from his pocket and tossed it to the gull, who snatched it up.

This is what he got for leaving his therapy group, for his hubris in thinking he could handle the rig fire's blowback without help. Sure, the long drive to Aberdeen was a pain, and the lady therapist far too saccharine for his taste, but at least that lot would have a clue how to approach dating again.

And what did he get for his stubborn pride? His night terrors returned with a vengeance. He'd rattled Addy, probably destroying her trust, and he could have hurt her too, a thought that filled him with sick dread.

With a weary sigh, he pulled his phone from his jacket pocket and re-read Addy's text for the umpteenth time.

> **Please don't let one bad dream come between us.**

Sweet of her to say, but there would be more bad dreams, lots of them. After the rig fire, it had been years before he had a solid night's sleep.

Maybe the surge of emotion he felt in Addy's arms triggered last night's nightmare. Or perhaps it was the ghost, or the phase of the moon, or who feckin' knows? Whatever the cause, he couldn't let night terrors take control of his life again, not when he'd finally found peace and a woman he wanted so badly.

"Who'da thought a crusty old fool like me would fall so hard for a doctor?" he asked the gull, who replied with a squawk. "Just one night with Addy, and I'm well and truly besotted. But she deserves a man who's whole and strong, not a broken mess who battles dream demons."

Even though he was a thousand percent sure their connection was the real deal, could a man as unstable as him dare to trust his feelings?

"Quit stalling, you fool." He pulled up his contact list and tapped the number he'd been avoiding for too long.

Getting a cell phone signal out on the beach was a hit-or-miss affair, but this time, his call went straight through.

"Aberdeen Therapy Center. How can I direct your call?"

He cleared his throat against a sudden tightness. "Is Candace Lew available?"

"I'm sorry, sir. Candace has moved to California. Is there anyone else you'd like to speak to?"

"Uh…" He pinched the bridge of his nose, nauseated at the prospect of starting this process all over again. "Has someone else taken over the PTSD support group?"

"Not at present. I can put you in touch with a resource line at the VA."

"I'm not a veteran," he grumbled and ended the call. Stiff with frustration, he kicked the sand, startling the gull, who flew away in a burst of mocking laughter.

Kieran's phone pinged in his hand. Another text from Addy:

> **I'm on my way. Snoot too. We're both worried about you.**

A flurry of sensations rushed through him—tingling excitement, a prickle of cold fear, and a wash of heat. But if he had a chance at fixing things after last night's cowardice, he'd better pull his arse together right quick.

> **I'm on the beach.**

He surveyed his surroundings—damn, he'd wandered far from home. In fact, he was closer to Addy's place than his own.

> **Meet you at the lifeguard station near the Narwhal Lane stairs.**

Three dots pulsed on his screen, then disappeared, then reappeared. At last, a thumbs-up emoji.

Well then, nothing to do but wait…and rehearse his apology.

Ten minutes later, a booming "Rowlf!" announced Snoot's approach, soon followed by the sand-crusted beast himself, wiggling from nose to tail with delight.

"Hello, fella. Good to see you." He squatted to ruffle the dog's fur.

"Easy, Snoot," Addy called as she trotted up to join them, each footfall kicking up a plume of sand.

God, she looked good. Fresh-faced, her cheeks glowing from the run—or perhaps from nerves as jittery as his? Her tight expression was hard to read as she swung a backpack off her shoulder and clutched it to her chest.

"I, uh, packed us lunch."

"It's nearly three, Addy."

She lifted her shoulder. "Seems we talk best over food, so..."

"Right. I, uh..." His mouth went desert dry, and words stuck in his throat. "Thank you. That's very kind of you." He glanced around for a sheltered spot.

"Kieran." She gripped his forearm gently, and the urgency in her voice yanked his gaze back to hers—as deep and green as the sea, a soulful stare that brooked no evasion. "I care about you. Let's not waste time with bullshit pleasantries."

Warmth bloomed in his chest. God, this woman! Direct and frank, and braver than he was by far.

"Agreed. And for the record, I care about you too."

"That's a good place to start." She rose onto her toes and pecked his lips. "Now, where shall we eat?"

He cast a glance at the shoreline and smiled. "I know just the spot."

He shouldered her backpack, and arm in arm they walked south, scattering little plovers before them on the mirror-smooth sand, until they reached the rock wall that marked the entrance to Ivan's Hollow, a secret cove accessible only at low tide. And right now, the tide was very low indeed. On a cool autumn day like this, they'd likely have the spot to themselves.

Grinning, he clasped Addy's hand. "Quick now, before the next wave soaks us." He broke into a run, towing her around the outcropping and into the secret beach known only to locals. Snoot sprinted ahead of them, splashing in the shallow surf.

When they trotted to a stop, Addy dropped his hand and pivoted in a slow circle, mouth agape as she drank in the U-shaped enclosure of slate-gray cliffs dotted with wind-twisted pines. Sugar-soft sand at their feet, gentle swells before them, and—as if cued by their arrival—a squadron of pelicans that flapped past in perfect formation, heading south.

Addy clasped her hands over her heart. "This is magical!"

"It's my favorite place."

While Snoot lowered his nose and wandered off to explore, Kieran led her to a log above the waterline where they sat while Addy unpacked their lunch: crusty rolls stuffed with meat, cheese, and vegetables, and dripping with oil and vinegar. "The love child of an Italian grinder and a New Orleans muffaletta. I hope you like it."

"You're too good to me, Addy." Armed with paper napkins, he took a big chomp. "Mmmf," he moaned around a mouthful of mortadella, salami, ham, provolone, and some kind of pickled vegetable relish.

She giggled. "Here, you've got olive salad in your beard." She dabbed at his chin with a napkin, and he gently seized her wrist. Better get it out now before he lost his nerve.

"Addy, love, I'm sorry. Truly I am. Last night was perfect until I spoiled it. I hadn't had a nightmare in a while, and I foolishly put that possibility out of mind because I wanted to spend the night in your arms." He flattened her palm over his heart. "I had no right to put you in danger."

Her eyes glowed with emotion. "Listen, since the moment we met, I've been completely honest with you. You know how rare that is for me? I usually keep the messy details to myself, but you make me feel comfortable and safe, and last night..." The tip of her tongue chased a drop of olive oil clinging to her lip. "You were right. Once with you is not enough."

Did she realize how her unconscious, sensual gestures drove him mad? His cock reared up, straining painfully against his zipper. But diving back into her bed wouldn't remove the obstacles between them.

Addy flushed and ducked her head. "I promise, I didn't come over here to jump your bones. I just want to clear the air and see if we can find our way past this." She took his hand and threaded her fingers through his. "I really hope we can. I could use a friend who understands what I've been through, someone I can talk to about the aftershocks, about how to rebuild a life after going through hell."

Her mouth said "friend," but the glimmer in her eye promised more.

"I wish I knew how to help you, Addy." He sighed and shook his head. "Since coming to Trappers Cove, I've been fooling myself. I thought I was putting the past behind me, but..." Damn, this was hard, but he had to push through for Addy's sake.

"I realize I've only been surviving, just skimming the surface," he continued. "Meeting you makes me want to dive deep, do the hard work, you know? But I'm afraid I'm too damaged to be the friend you deserve."

There it was, the truth in all its ugliness. Heart hammering, he waited for her to take it up—or turn away.

Addy scooted closer, pressing her thigh to his—an intoxicating distraction. "I don't need a perfect partner, Kieran, just someone I can open up to."

A sudden lightness filled his body, fizzing like champagne and hope. He raised her hand to his lips. "That I can do."

The way her pupils flared at the touch of his mouth on her skin...Jaysus!

"So, I have a confession," she continued, extricating her hand. "I've been dodging therapy."

"You? But you're so brave, Addy."

She flashed a wry grin. "I did what needed to be done. I didn't really have a choice." She pinched off a chunk of bread from her sandwich and pitched it toward their growing audience of hopeful seagulls. "Funny how, once you have a degree behind your name, people think you've got it all figured out. I don't, Kieran, not at all."

"What have you tried?"

She winced, wrinkling her nose adorably. "I've been relying on my friend Liv, which isn't fair to her. She's got a crazy-busy cascload, but the therapist assigned to me..." She circled her wrist, searching for words. "He sets me on edge. His eyes remind me of a shark's—flat, unemotional. And he mostly just repeats what I say, as if that's supposed to cure me. So I tried a support group on base, but..." She crumpled her napkin, evading his gaze. "It's held during the duty day, so I had to attend in uniform, and...it got awkward. All these young guys in combat specialties, and here's me, a pampered doctor, and old enough to be their mom."

"Can you request a different therapist?"

"That'd be selfish of me. So many people need therapy, and there aren't enough mental health practitioners to help them all."

"I see." He looped his arm around her waist, snugging her closer. "Sounds like you need to find support off the base."

Chuckling, she nudged him with her shoulder. "It never occurred to me to look. We military folks can be kind of insular, I guess. See? That's why I need your perspective."

"Glad to help, ma'am." He gave her knee a squeeze. "And since we're confessing, I've been dodging therapy too."

"Is there someone you can see here?"

He shook his head. "The hospital—really, it's more of a clinic—anyway, they lost their last psych doc a while ago. There's a family therapist, but she mostly works with kids."

"Huh." She paused to attack her sandwich again, chewing thoughtfully as she stared out to sea. The seagull squad tap-danced closer, hoping for another handout.

The words pushed hard, itching to escape Kieran's lips. *Stay here, Addy. With me. Our community needs more doctors...and I need you.* Before he could blurt out something so audacious, and probably scare her away for good, he stuffed his mouth with more delicious sandwich.

"Tell you what," she said at last after tossing the remnants of her meal to the hungry gulls, "when I get back home, I'll do some research. There must be support groups between Fort Lewis-McChord and here."

Home. Wherever that was for Addy, it wasn't here. His stomach sank like a stone in a pond. That's what he got for spinning foolish fantasies.

"Thanks, Doc. That's kind of you." He hoped he didn't sound as gloomy as he felt, because the threat of her departure blotted all the joy from this sweet moment.

"Hey." Her soft hand closed over his and squeezed with surprising strength. "Look at me, Kieran. Please."

He did, lips pressed tightly together to quell their wobble. Addy cupped his cheek. "I don't know what to do about us. My life is such a..." She chuckled. "Well, I shouldn't use such language around you."

"Go ahead. Whatever it is, I've heard worse."

The corners of her mouth ticked up. "Fine. My life is such a clusterfuck, I don't know which way is up, and I may not for some time. But if you're patient with me, we'll figure it out together, okay?"

Addy's probing gaze searched his for reassurance and, in that luminous moment, he could no more resist kissing her than he could stop his own heartbeat. Stroking his fingers into her hair, he lowered his mouth to hers.

"We'll find a way," he whispered into their kiss. "Together."

With a resounding woof, Snoot barreled toward them, scattering the seagulls as he zoomed in circles around the log where they sat. His protective duty completed, he plopped onto the sand at their feet and stared avidly at the remains of Kieran's sandwich.

"Can he have a bit of ham?" Kieran asked.

Laughing, Addy nodded her assent. "You're going to spoil him, you know."

"Give me a chance, and I'll spoil both of you." He tossed a scrap to the Lab, then nuzzled Addy's neck. "But right now, the tide is turning, and the wind's picking up. Any chance I can talk you into continuing this discussion at my place?"

She arched her throat, inviting more kisses. Her pulse galloped beneath his lips. "Right now," she purred, "there's nowhere else I'd rather be."

Right now, Doc? What will it take to turn right now into forever?

Chapter Thirteen

♥

Dusk stained the sky deep indigo by the time they stumbled up to Kieran's cottage, laughing and kissing and fumbling at each other's clothing.

When Kieran kicked the door open, Addy's heart skittered. And when he swept her into his powerful arms, pressed her against the wall, and plundered her mouth, she forgot how to breathe.

Unconcerned with the humans' gyrations, Snoot snuffled his way into the cottage, nose to the ground, tail wagging. From the corner of her eye, Addy saw him hop onto a loveseat by the fireplace and nestle into the cushions.

"Snoot, down," she commanded. "You're a sandy mess." But the dog only stared, his brow contracted in a canine plea.

"Let him be," Kieran murmured into her hair. "I'll clean up later. Besides, the sofa's too small for what I want to do with you."

"Yikes!" she squealed when he tunneled his icy hands inside her jeans and gave her ass a squeeze. "Are you trying to stop my heart?"

"Quite the opposite, beauty." But he obligingly removed his chilly digits and strode across the living room to light the fireplace. As soon as flames licked the logs, he turned to her, desire smoldering in his gaze. "Music, love?" He glanced at Snoot, sprawled and basking in the fire's warmth. "It might distract our friend here from any noises we make."

Closing the distance between them, he settled his hands on her hips, and murmured into her ear, "Be warned, beauty. I plan to make some noise with you tonight."

"Music would be great," she whispered, leaning into his hold. What kind of music did a hunky Irish lighthouse keeper listen to? Celtic flutes? Irish fiddles?

Kieran tapped his phone, and bluesy piano notes filled the room as Annie Lennox crooned, "I put a spell on you..."

Addy gave a throaty laugh and wound her arms around his neck. "Not what I would have guessed."

He slid his broad hand between her shoulder blades and swayed her to the lazy, sensual beat. "I like the way we surprise each other."

"Amen." She raised her lips for another kiss.

Dancing her backwards, Kieran licked into her mouth, his tongue a velvety marvel that flooded her core with heat. Heavens above, this man! Instinctively, he knew exactly how to tease her higher, hotter, loosening her body until she flowed like honey in his arms.

Their slow tango ended when Addy's back met the cool, smooth wood of his bedroom door.

"Addy," he breathed, his forehead pressed to hers. "Do you know how I've dreamed and wished and prayed you'd end up here in my bed?"

He grasped her thigh and pulled it to his waist, angling his hips so the hard ridge of his erection scraped the seam of her jeans. Pleasure ricocheted through her, sizzling along her nerves.

And then her feet left the floor. Clutching her ass, he leaned into her, all firm muscle and hot skin and deep, rumbling moans. Hands clasped behind his neck, she held on tight as he rocked his hips in rhythm with his plundering tongue.

"Kieran," she gasped, "if you don't stop soon, I'm going to come right here."

He chuckled into her mouth. "Would that be a bad thing, beauty?"

"But I want to feel you." She tore at his flannel shirt. "All of you."

With a sexy grunt, he released her, groaning when she slid down his front. He opened the door, but before she could get a proper look at his bedroom, he scooped her up and carried her to his bed, an old-fashioned four-poster affair sturdy enough for the roughest play.

A shiver ran through her as he gently set her down and tugged off her shoes and socks.

"Crap, sorry," she said as sand pattered onto the wooden floor.

"We were both distracted. I'll sweep up later." A wolfish grin lit his face as he made quick work of the rest of her clothes until she lay spread out naked on his soft patchwork quilt, her skin prickling with goosebumps. His glittering eyes drank in her body as he swiftly shed his own clothing and stood before her, his stance wide, his fat, ruddy cock jutting upward.

She reached for him, but he pushed her onto the mattress, then knelt between her splayed thighs to grip her knees and spread them wider. "Look at you," he gritted out. "You're magnificent."

He dove in, sealing his mouth to her sex in a deep, suckling kiss. Addy squirmed away from sensations almost too sharp to bear, but he pursued her relentlessly, the two of them thrashing across the mattress until her head collided with the carved headboard.

Kieran rose on his knees, captured her wrists in a firm grip, and crouched above her, his eyes blazing. "Stay right here."

His commanding tone stoked her arousal even higher. This man was full of delicious surprises. Come what may, she had to find a way to hold on to this dizzying ride until its inevitable end.

"Be here now," she muttered under her breath. This was not the time to think about endings, not with her body thrumming with need and Kieran returning from his antique wardrobe clutching a fistful of...

"Neckties?"

"Best I can do on short notice." Eyes blazing, he stroked the silk over her bare skin, a whispery sensation that contrasted deliciously with his rough growl. "Since my lady has a hard time holding still..." He cocked an eyebrow and flashed a wicked grin.

For a moment, she stared, baffled, and then his meaning landed like a heat bomb between her legs. She'd never done this before, but the thought of lying wide open, completely at his mercy, shot a throb of searing heat through her core.

She nodded her consent.

The mattress dipped as he climbed aboard and, as skillfully as any seasoned sailor, knotted them together, and fastened her spread-eagled to the bedposts.

"That's better, my squirmy love. No more trying to escape before I've given you all the pleasure you can take." Eyes lust-dark, swollen cock crowned with a crystalline tear, he lowered his head to her belly and circled her navel with the tip of his tongue. "What will you tell me if you want me to stop?"

"Umm..." She'd never in her life been asked for a safe word. "How about 'Nebraska'?"

His laughter tickled her skin, making her squirm—but not far. She lay helpless before his merciless mouth and hands and glorious cock. Pleasure flowed through her, knowing she was Kieran's to play with until they were both satisfied.

His hot, wet mouth made a complete tour of her body, teasing her just to the edge before he rose again to claim another drugging kiss. While his lips and tongue worked magic on her nipples, she heard a drawer open, then the crackle of a foil packet. Just when she thought she'd ignite from anticipation, he lowered his hips to hers. The plump, wide head of his cock probed her tingling folds, and she nearly levitated off the bed, eyes shut tight against the delirious intensity.

"Addy, love, look at me."

She obeyed, sinking into his fiery gaze.

"I need to feel you coming around my cock. Are you ready for me?"

Biting her lip hard, she nodded and canted her hips, chasing the fullness she craved.

That first slow glide melted her bones. The world beyond Kieran's bed faded and blurred until all she knew was his touch, his breath, his weight driving her into the mattress. Overpowering pleasure unfurled, licking her skin like flame with each thrust until her climax detonated in brilliant waves of joy. With a ragged roar, Kieran slammed into her once, twice, then froze as his own release seized him.

He collapsed atop her, panting and slick with sweat, and Addy was filled with so much tenderness, her eyes stung with happy tears.

But Kieran was a big man, and soon her lungs protested his weight.

"Nebraska," she whispered.

He immediately rolled off her, taking his half-erect cock with him. She sighed at the loss.

"Did I hurt you?" He ran his hand over her skin, searching for injuries.

"Not at all. But you're kind of heavy." She tugged at her silken restraints. "And I'd like my hands back, please."

"Of course, love." He quickly untied the knots and gently massaged her wrists.

Grabbing a silk necktie, she looped it around his neck and pulled him down for a kiss. "I like this game. My turn next time?"

His smile glowed with satisfaction. "There'll be a next time, then?"

"Several, if I have my way."

"Oh, Addy." He wrapped his arms around her and rolled onto his back, draping her limp, sated body over him like a blanket. His voice rumbled against her cheek. "Can an accomplished beauty like you ever learn to love a wreck of a man like me?"

"Hey." She rose on her elbow and fixed him with a stern glare. "You are not broken."

His lips quirked in a wry grin. "I notice you didn't answer the question."

Damn. He wasn't going to let her evade this time.

She traced spirals through his russet chest hair. "I told you before, I'm not good at making quick decisions. We've only known each other a few days, and—"

His expression flattened. "I get it. I'm asking for too much."

He rolled away and sat on the edge of the bed, his back to her—his scar-slashed back, broad and strong and bowed under the pain she'd caused. "Guess I got carried away. Forget I asked."

She popped onto her knees and wrapped her arms around him, her chin on his shoulder. "No, I won't forget. Because what I feel for you is stronger than anything I've felt since my life fell apart. Our worlds are so different, Kieran, but this I do know—I care for you deeply, and I'm not ready to say goodbye."

He turned into her embrace, his eyes glassy-bright. "Well, that's a start, anyway." He kissed the top of her head and gestured to his glistening, latex-covered cock. "I'll go clean up and make us some tea. You rest."

She sank onto the pillows. "This could be my home," she whispered, daring to speak aloud the thought that had danced on the edge of her imagination since their first night together.

After leaving Nebraska for college, then medical school, then seven different postings in sixteen years, not to mention her two tours in Afghanistan, home was a a slippery feeling she tried to capture by hanging the same few photos on new walls, putting new wildflowers in her grandmother's milk-glass vase. But over the years, the sense of home became more and more elusive, replaced by an aching, empty space inside her.

What would it be like to really sink roots? To hang up those photos knowing she wouldn't be taking them down anytime soon?

An electric kettle hissed in the kitchen. Kieran would be back in a moment, and he deserved an honest answer. If only she knew what that was. Zora the fortuneteller spoke of a new perspective, of learning from the past...

Addy's eyes drifted closed, then opened again when the mattress dipped. She pushed up onto her elbows. "Kieran, I—"

The next words stuck in her throat. Kieran wasn't there, but someone was—a vague, pale outline that solidified as Addy gawked, her heart thundering.

"Mary?" she whispered.

The specter tilted her head and regarded Addy with dark, soulful eyes. But instead of the aching sadness she'd felt at their last encounter, the ghost radiated calm—and perhaps interest?

"Can you see me, Mary?"

The ghost drifted forward and wrapped her transparent hand around the bedpost at Addy's feet. Her voice seemed to come from far away. "We were happy here."

When the bedroom door opened to Kieran, dressed in flannel pajama pants and carrying a tray, Mary vanished.

"Addy? You all right?"

She could only splutter incoherently and point to the foot of the bed.

He set the tray on the nightstand, sat beside her, and took her hand. "Your fingers are like ice, love. Here." He drew the quilt over her goosebump-pebbled skin.

"She was here," Addy choked out. "Did you see her?"

Brow rumpled, he tilted his head. "Who was here?"

"Mary. The ghost. The White Widow. She was standing right there." She gulped hard. "She spoke to me."

Kieran slung his arm around her shoulders and drew her against his bare chest. "I've never seen her in the cottage. Makes sense, though, since her home was here." He cupped her jaw in both hands. "Did she upset you?"

Shivering, she shook her head. "I don't think she meant me any harm."

"What did she say?"

"I...I'm not sure. Maybe I was just dreaming and didn't realize it." She didn't quite understand her reluctance to share, except for a nagging sense the message was for her alone.

Kieran poured her a mug of fragrant tea and pressed it into her hands. "Drink up. If you want, I'll drive you home."

She sipped and breathed in apple-spice scented steam, cozy and sweet.

Perhaps their lovemaking had stirred up Mary's spirit. The poor soul was trapped here, eternally searching for her lost love. And Addy had found what Mary lost—the love of a good man who understood her more deeply than any man ever had. But Kieran was hurting, and her hesitation added to his pain.

She set down her mug and touched his cheek. "If you don't mind, I'd like to stay."

Chapter Fourteen

♥

By four a.m., Kieran gave up. Sleep was a lost cause. The irony burned in his gut. Just when he'd found the perfect companion to brighten what had been a lonely shell of a life, just when happiness dangled before his eyes like a tantalizing jewel...

After the most soul-quaking sex of his forty-seven years, he held Addy in his arms, sleepy-soft, unguarded, her lashes fanned against her delicate cheekbones. For hours he drank her in, praying her comforting presence would keep the terrors away. Was one night of sweet dreams too much to ask?

Apparently so, because he jolted awake at two a.m. with fire licking his back like a hungry demon and screams of the dying ringing in his ears. Worst of all, he saw Jack Jefferson's face pressed against the window of the control house, eyes wide in pain and terror. And then the glass shattered, and Jack was gone.

Biting his lip so hard he drew blood, he stifled a scream and bolted from the bed.

He mustn't let Addy see how damaged he was. She had troubles enough of her own—a burden he couldn't begin to imagine.

And so, here he sat, high atop the lighthouse, clutching a mug of cold tea and watching dawn lift the darkness from the sea.

Steps clanged on the metal stairs below. She'd found his note, then. He steeled himself for the hard talk to come. What an eejit he'd been, thinking he had anything to offer Addy.

Her soft hand gently gripped his shoulder. "Couldn't sleep?"

He turned to find her expression relaxed and unguarded. She held a thermos and a mug. "The kettle was cold, so I figured you'd been up for a while. I made us a fresh pot." She pulled up a folding chair and sat beside him. "Though I've got to say, your super-strong Irish breakfast tea will take some getting used to."

He couldn't help but smile, despite expecting the worst. "Sorry, love. Believe me, I'd rather be in bed with you than up here."

She refilled his mug with dark, steaming tea. "I believe you." She poured her own cuppa, stretched out her legs, and sighed. "New perspective."

"Pardon?"

She kept her gaze on the horizon as she spoke. "That's what Zora said I needed. Time to re-evaluate my life, learn from it, and forge a new path." She ducked her chin and gave a sheepish grin. "Something like that. I wrote it all down in my journal." She took a sip and winced. "You ever consider getting a coffee machine?"

"Addy—" He swiveled to face her, elbows on his knees.

"Bad dream again?" she asked, holding his gaze.

He searched her jade eyes but found no trace of bitterness, no judgment, just calm, open curiosity.

"Yeah. You were sleeping so peacefully, and I didn't want to spoil the moment, so I..." Easier to stare at his boots than see disappointment clouding her eyes. "Surrendered to the inevitable, I suppose."

"Hey." She set down her mug and gripped his knee. "Look at me, Kieran."

He cracked a mirthless grin. "My favorite pastime."

"We're both haunted, you and I." Her eyes glittered, keen and bright in the low, gray light. "I hear mortar fire when a car backfires, screams of the dying when children play. It's been a long, hard slog back to safety, and the journey's not over yet."

"And now, you're seeing ghosts in my bed." He took her hand and squeezed it. "And I can't sleep without reliving it all." He shifted his gaze to the pale, silvery sea. "I thought I'd put it all behind me, Addy. But it seems meeting you..." Dread hollowed his chest. This wasn't going to work between them. Between his nightmares and her impossible choices, there was no room for love to grow.

"It's stirred up some powerful feelings." She wove her fingers through his, and a tiny flicker of hope winked back to life. "If we have to sleep apart until the dust settles, so be it." She lifted his hand to her heart and pressed it there, over the steady thump thump he felt even through her wool sweater and windbreaker. "I'm not afraid of ghosts, Kieran—not mine, not yours, and not poor Mary."

Well, well, perhaps he'd been too quick to expect the worst. His Addy was a strong one, and he'd do well to emulate her.

From far below, a deep woof sounded.

Addy huffed a laugh and rose to her feet. "Snoot's up."

"Right." He drained his cup. "And I need to open up for visitors soon. So—" He stood and pulled her into a tight hug. "Thank you, Addy."

"For the tea?"

"For not giving up on me when I nearly gave up on myself."

She took his face in her hands. "I may be slow to decide, Kieran, but I've already made one choice. This thing we've found together is worth fighting for."

She pecked his lips, then trotted down the stairs, her footfalls ringing out like a musical scale.

Kieran lingered for a moment, staring out to sea as he conjured the face of his mentor. "Jack, at your funeral, I promised to pass on the kindness you showed me, but I've been too focused on my own hurt to do much good for others. It's time to change that, and I've found the woman who'll help me do it—if I can convince her to stick around."

"Can I help you find anything in particular?" The fifty-something red-haired knockout flashed a welcoming smile.

Sure, Addy thought, *I'd like a big, fat neon sign pointing me in the right direction. And a solution to Kieran's nightmares. And a pet unicorn, while I'm at it.*

"I'm looking for a Halloween costume. For the party at Salty Dog Saloon."

"Oh, you're coming to Ryan and Lilo's party?" She beamed. "New in town? I'm Annie, by the way."

"I figured as much." The sign above the door read *Annie's Vintage Treasures*, and in her 1950s black and white polka dot frock, its wide collar accented by a sparkly jack-o'-lantern brooch—this woman was a walking advertisement for vintage fashion. Had Addy ever worn something so deliciously flashy?

"Vintage fashion is my passion." Annie grinned. "Benefit of being the owner—I get to snap up the best pieces." She extended her hand. "And you are?"

"Addy Connor. I'm just here for the week, but—" Uh oh, would Kieran want his neighbors to know they were dating? There was so much about him she didn't know. "Someone invited me to the party, and it sounds like fun."

"It'll be an absolute blast. Come, let's see what we can find." She took Addy's arm and towed her toward the women's clothing section. Other antiques shops were dominated by out-of-date furniture and kitschy glassware, but half of this large emporium was taken up by racks of garments from cocktail hats to tuxedos, shoes from 1920s-style spats to 1970s disco platforms, and cases of colorful costume jewelry. A peacock's paradise, and so different from Addy's usual functional, outdoorsy look, it made her want to try something daring.

"Soooo." Annie rubbed her hands together, her pretty face alight. "What are you feeling this Halloween? With your dark hair, you'd make a lovely Audrey Hepburn." She held up a classic little black dress. "Or a groovy hippie chick?" She displayed a fringed suede vest. "Or a zombie bride? I've got lots of bridal gowns." She continued, flipping through the racks until she came to a white lab coat. "Or a sexy doctor?"

Addy laughed. "No thanks. That's my day job—the doctor part, not the sexy part."

Annie raised an eyebrow and gave her a quick up and down glance. "Think again, doll. Okay, something wider afield." She turned to a display of lace curtains. "How about a ghost? We have a local one, the White Widow. Someone always turns up dressed like her."

There was no way Addy would dress up as that poor, tortured woman. "No thanks." She pointed to a ruffled red blouse. "This looks promising."

Annie's grin widened. "Oh, yes. Excellent. This color is great with your skin tone. Now, where are we going with this? Flamenco dancer? Fortuneteller?"

Addy plucked a black satin skirt from the rack. "Pirate wench?"

"Love it!" Annie crowed. "Let's accessorize."

While Annie scurried off, Addy felt a buzz in her pocket. Right, she'd left her phone on silent so as not to wake Kieran—a useless precaution, as it turned out. She fished it out, tapped Accept Call, and her best friend's smiling face filled the screen.

"Liv! What's up?"

"Girl, today has been *a day*. I need a shot of sanity. Show me your beach town."

"I'm actually in a vintage shop, picking out my Halloween costume."

"Annie's place? I love that store!" Liv's cackle shot a pang of loss through Addy. What was she going to do without her friend's laughter? Liv had another six years to go before retirement and planned to ride it out with the Army, which meant she'd be transferred somewhere else.

"Ah ah ah," Liv scolded. "No boo-boo lip, young lady. Quit your pouting and show me something pretty."

Addy turned the screen around and pivoted slowly.

"Ooo, those cocktail hats! I'll take the one with the blue feathers. I've gotta get my ass out to Trappers Cove. It's been too long. Now, seriously—" Like flipping a switch, Liv dropped her playful tone. "I bumped into Colonel Okafor. She told me about the accelerated deadline. Are you any closer to a decision?"

"Maybe. I..." She threw a glance over her shoulder and spotted Annie with an armful of colorful cloth.

"Take your time," Annie called and pointed to a velvet loveseat near the window.

Addy sank down and lowered her voice. "Yes and no."

"Nope, huh-uhn. None of that wishy-washy bullshit. I need specifics," Liv demanded.

"Well, I'm closing in on what I don't want: Nebraska."

"Duh." Liv wrinkled her nose. "Your family is a classic case of toxic parents not wanting their children to outshine them." She scowled and stabbed the screen with her forefinger. "If you let those shit-stirring fools reel you back in, I'll have to haul my overworked ass out to the cornfields and drag you home."

Addy huffed a laugh. "Yeah, but where is home?"

"Trappers Cove looks good on you. You've got a glow, girlfriend. Something you're not telling me?"

It felt damn good to laugh this hard. Wherever Addy landed, she'd need a friend like Liv in her life.

"Okay, okay—I met a guy."

"And?" Liv's eyebrows danced up and down. "Is he keeper material?"

"As close as I've come in forever." She checked to make sure Annie was safely out of hearing range. "But he and I are in the same boat."

"He's military?"

"No, but he's been through something rough. An oil rig fire. Nearly died. Lost a lot of friends."

Liv gave a low whistle. "So you both have PTSD? Ay ay ay."

"Terrible idea, right?"

Her friend waggled a hand. "Could be challenging. Could also be helpful—I mean, who's going to understand your quirks better than someone who's going through something similar?"

Addy snorted. "Quirks? I freak out at loud noises, and he has night terrors."

"Right. That might make it hard for a normie to cope, but someone as strong and compassionate as you..."

She was doing that trailing-off-and-looking-at-the-ceiling thing she did when she wanted Addy to draw a certain conclusion, and Addy didn't have time for that.

"But with someone like me...what?"

"It's a coin toss, darlin'. Depends on the two people involved. I don't know him, but I know you, and you've been hiding your needs behind work and duty for far too long. If you've found someone who helps you stop hiding, well...it's worth a considering."

Addy blew out a long breath. "Okay. I'll think on it. And thanks. I miss you."

"Miss you too, love." In the background, a loudspeaker blared a staticky announcement. "Shit. Meeting. Gotta go. Mwah!"

Addy blew a kiss and ended the call.

A few minutes later, she left the vintage shop lighter of heart—and wallet—and laden with floppy boots, a red scarf, a wide belt, the blouse and skirt, skull and crossbones earrings, and a shiny plastic sword, plus the blue, feathered cocktail chapeau for Liv.

"Arrgh," she snarled in her best pirate accent, grinning as she peeked into her shopping bag. "Kieran won't know what hit him."

Chapter Fifteen

♥

Addy was putting the finishing touches on her pirate costume when a loud knock on her door caused her to fumble her scarlet lipstick.

"Trick or treat!"

Huh. Most of the little goblins had come between six and seven, and that voice sounded pretty grown-up to be trick or treating. Must be the teens' turn at candy-grubbing. Good thing she had plenty of baby Snickers and Twizzlers left.

She grabbed the candy bowl and opened the door to a beloved face, tinted green and topped with a pointy witch's cap.

"Surprise!" Liv flung her arms wide and enveloped Addy in a tight, squishy hug. "Happy Halloween, lovey!"

"Liv!" Fizzing with delight, she rocked her bestie back and forth.

"I decided the drive was worth it for a well-earned break. My first appointment isn't until ten tomorrow, so..." She shimmied her abundant boobs, tightly encased in a nylon witch costume that threatened to split under the load. "Fabulous costume, Ads. Let's party! Where's the wine?"

Addy bustled her friend inside and poured her a glass of the fruity rose she'd picked up from the Food Co-op in case tonight's party didn't end as she'd hoped, along with supplies for a sumptuous breakfast, in case it did.

"Aren't you drinking?" Liv asked when Addy filled her own wineglass with raspberry seltzer. Her eyes narrowed, then widened. "Oh my God, are you—"

"No no no!" Addy's cheeks heated. The Kieran question was complicated enough without this layer. "My new friend, he's sort of..."

Liv arched one perfectly painted eyebrow. "In recovery?"

"Let's just say he has good reasons not to drink. And I figure this week's mission is better tackled with a clear head, so I'm abstaining too. But you go ahead."

"I will." They clinked glasses, and Liv took a healthy gulp. "So, where's this Halloween bash?"

"Salty Dog Saloon. Have you been there?"

"Not for years. You?"

Addy fiddled with the buckle on her 1980s slouchy suede boot. "I've been busy with other things."

"Like making new friends?" Liv's conspiratorial grin lit up her sparkly green face. "Can't wait to meet him. When's he picking you up?"

"We're meeting at the party, actually. Said he had a last-minute errand to take care of."

"Very mysterious." Liv tweaked a glitter-sprayed curl behind Addy's ear, then tugged her boho blouse lower over one shoulder. "Good to see you letting your adventurous side come out to play."

If you only knew. Thrilled as she was to have Liv here, her presence put a damper on plans to spend the night with Kieran, and she'd spent the afternoon imagining the gleam in his hazel eyes as he peeled her boots off her legs and buried his head beneath her satin skirt.

But she couldn't ask Liv to get a room elsewhere, not when she'd driven all this way.

After tonight, that left only two more nights with Kieran before her leave ended. Not enough time, damn it. There were so many questions she needed to ask him, so many possibilities to discuss.

But tonight was not for spinning her mental wheels. Tonight was to be enjoyed. And if it brought together two people she loved, so much the better.

Love? Addy's stomach swooped.

Last night, Kieran asked if she could ever love a man like him, and tonight she'd tell him she already did—because nothing else explained the keen ache that stabbed between her ribs every time she contemplated her departure, or the way his steady presence instantly relaxed her, even while confessing the worst experiences of her life. She meant what she promised last night. She had no intention of leaving him behind.

"You okay, hon?" Liv tilted her head and regarded Addy with that cool, analytical gaze that saw right through her defensive bullshit.

"I will be." She flashed a tight, determined smile. "Come on, let's go shake up this little town."

"Woo-ee, these coastal folks know how to party," Liv crowed as they reached Salty Dog Saloon's street-facing deck. A large fire-pit table blazed brightly, surrounded by ghouls, witches, a sexy she-devil, and a pair of trolls in neon-colored shock wigs, all of them rowdy and loud. On the far side of the deck, costumed patrons bowled plastic skulls toward pins painted like ghosts. Servers dressed as zombies wove through the crowd, fully loaded trays held high, while Warren Zevon's "Werewolves of London" blared from speakers on posts decked with blinking orange and purple lights.

Liv grabbed Addy's hand and plunged into the melee, exclaiming at costumes as they made their way to the bar. "Check out the aliens!" She pointed to a cute couple in silver face paint and metallic spacesuits. "And what even is that?" She indicated a guy bopping past, covered from neck to knees in Post-its, with tissue-paper streamers in his hair.

"I'm a piñata, love," he sang out and raised his margarita glass. "Salud!"

While they waited their turn at the bustling bar, manned by a handsome blond mummy in a shredded tux and a dark-haired lady vampire in a figure-hugging red dress, someone tugged on Addy's sleeve. It was Zora, the psychic from the crystal shop, in a green tunic trimmed with fake leaves and crooked coat-hanger wings, beside a taller woman wearing a *Read Banned Books* T-shirt, a tutu made of rolled book pages, and wings made from the cover of an old dictionary.

"Happy Halloween, Doctor Addy!" Zora shouted above the din. "How's that malachite working for you?"

"Oh, uh—"

Beside her, Liv giggled. "Fabulous costumes, ladies. Let me guess—you're a forest fairy, and you're a..."

"Book fairy." The taller woman gripped Liv's hand, then Addy's. "I'm Marquetta, Zora's wife and Trappers Cove's librarian." She tapped her chest and grinned. "Obviously, right? Are you two new in town, or just visiting?"

"Alas, Doctor Addy's just passing through." Zora heaved a dramatic sigh.

"We both work in the hospital on Joint Base Lewis-McChord," Liv explained.

"Military doctors, huh?" Marquetta gave them an appraising glance. "Sounds stressful. Keep us in mind when you retire, eh? TC Hospital has a hard time holding onto doctors."

Liv draped her arm over Addy's shoulders. "Sorry, I've got six more years to serve, but my friend here might be persuaded if the offer's tempting enough."

Addy elbowed her, but Liv only laughed.

"Oh, we'd love to hold onto Addy." Zora nodded vigorously. "She has a wise mind and a good heart."

She got that from one tarot reading?

"Amen," Liv declared. "After all she's been through, our Addy could use a peaceful home." She nudged Addy's ribs. "One with a spare room so I can visit her from my next duty station."

A shiver ran down Addy's spine as she drew Liv away from the nosy couple. "You got orders?" Liv had already extended her tour at Fort Lewis-McChord an extra six months, and Addy was dreading her departure.

"Got the news yesterday. Bassett Army Hospital, Fort Wainwright, Alaska." She hugged Addy closely. "I wanted to tell you in person."

"But that's so far!" Addy wailed. "God, I need a drink."

But before she could order one, a warm, heavy hand gripped her shoulder.

"What's your pleasure, my buccaneer queen?"

Liv's eyes bugged out. "Holy pirate's booty."

Kieran's deep, rumbly chuckle stirred Addy's hair and heated her core. She spun to embrace him—and stumbled backward at the sight of the sexiest swashbuckler ever to sail the seven seas. From his tricorn hat to his velveteen coat, lace jabot, snug breeches, and floppy boots, her keeper was every inch the seductive pirate captain.

Eyes smoldering, he likewise inspected her from head to booted toe.

Liv clamped onto Addy's arm. "Introduce me to your friend, Ads."

"Kieran Gallagher, meet my friend Liv Williams."

"Enchanted, Ms. Liv." He doffed his hat and swooped low in a theatrical bow.

"Is this the—" Liv whispered far too loudly.

"Yeah."

"You lucky girl." Liv smacked Addy's arm. "And you match perfectly. If you don't win the costume contest, I'll eat my pointy hat."

Kieran slung his arm over Addy's shoulder in a possessive gesture that thrilled her down to the red satin panties she'd hoped to show him later.

"Before I met Addy, I wasn't even planning to come out tonight, but..." He nuzzled Addy's sparkly hair. "My brother in Toronto? His girlfriend does costumes for a movie studio up there. She express-mailed this getup. That's why I'm late. Had to wait for the delivery truck."

"Fred," the blond bartender hollered, "Long time no see. Haven't seen you since the Labor Day carnival. What are you drinking?"

"Your finest ginger beer, please. And the ladies will have..." He turned to Addy and Liv.

"The same for me," Addy said.

"Rosé, please," Liv added, still gawking at Kieran. "Why'd he call you Fred?"

"Ah. Well, there's a story." Kieran stroked his beard. "When I came to the States, I got tired of being called 'Karen,' so I picked a name those roughneck lunkheads could pronounce."

Addy squeezed his biceps through his dashing coat. "Maybe it's time to unveil the real you."

"Look who's talking." Liv snorted a laugh. "Excuse me, you two." She pointed toward the back of the bar. "I haven't played beer pong since med school. I'm gonna go check it out." She moved toward a table in the corner where patrons bounced ping-pong balls into plastic pumpkins.

That was Liv, always noticing undercurrents. She'd given her and Kieran space to enjoy each other's company—not that they'd get much privacy in this merry mob.

"Fred!" A mustachioed older gent in a vampire cape thumped Kieran on the back as he passed. "Got your favorite

Amarena gelato back in stock. Come see us." He waggled his bushy eyebrows. "And bring your lady."

"Sal Verducci, meet Addy Connor, my—" Kieran raised an eyebrow, waiting for her to fill in the term she preferred.

"Girlfriend," she blurted. Well, why not? It was true, for the moment at least.

The old gent beamed. "You picked a good one, Miss Addy. This guy's a gem. When our generator died in the middle of the 4th of July street fair, he patched it up right quick."

"Glad to help, signore." Kieran slung his arm around Addy's waist and drew her away.

"Girlfriend, eh?" He snugged her close. "I like the sound of that."

"Sounds a little silly at our age, but if you're up for a long-distance, weekends-only thing…"

He crooked a finger under her chin and lifted her gaze to his. "Sounds perfect." He kissed her softly. "Though be forewarned, I hope to lure you here on a more permanent basis."

Shimmering inside with hope and happiness, she smiled into his kiss. "I'll add that to my list of possibilities."

Shouts from the bar's entrance interrupted their happy canoodling.

"Pretty rowdy tonight, even for a Halloween party." Addy rose on tiptoe to see what all the ruckus was about.

One by one, revelers drifted toward the door. The cries outside grew louder and more urgent, and soon the male bartender grabbed a baseball bat, shouted for his partner to call 911, then sprinted to the exit.

"Well, shit. Better go help." Kieran kissed her forehead and headed for the exit, with Addy close behind.

Outside, in the middle of Main Street, a scruffy white-haired man wielding a broken beer bottle charged back and forth, menacing anyone who came near. For an old guy, he had amazing speed, and the wild look in his eye set Addy's nerves on edge. She'd seen that look before, when a combat soldier, triggered by a sudden shock and fueled by adrenalin, tumbled into his own inner hell.

Sprawled on the ground, a man in a gruesome horror-movie villain costume clutched his abdomen and writhed in pain, while another guy with gory Halloween makeup dodged the attacker's thrusts, stupidly trying to knock the broken bottle out of the older man's hands.

"Fuckin' V-C! You killed my brother, but you ain't takin' me!" The attacker lunged and slashed, ripping a gash in the younger man's palm.

The wounded man tripped and tumbled backward, real blood mixing with fake as the old guy tackled him.

Kieran, the bartender, and a dozen other partygoers dove in, pinning the old man's arms and yanking the bottle from his hands, but the guy continued to rave and buck as they wrestled him to the ground.

Thankful she hadn't ordered that drink, Addy sped into the fray with Liv on her heels. While Liv knelt beside the attacker and tried to gentle him out of his flashback, Addy shouted instruction. The second monster to fall could wait, but the first one had a deep stab wound dangerously close to his liver.

Calm descended over Addy as her training kicked in.

"I need clean cloths. You—" She pointed to a pink Care Bear. "Run to the bar. Get me bottled water and clean towels. And you—" She indicated the Spandex superhero at her side. "Get me the bar's first aid kit."

Carefully, she peeled off the victim's creepy mask to reveal a pale young man shivering so hard his teeth chattered. "Am I gonna die?" he whimpered.

Considering the growing pool of blood he lay in, that was a very real possibility. She lifted his shirt to find a deep puncture wound welling with dark blood.

Crap, this was bad. What were the chances that, when this guy was donning his scary getup, he foresaw ending his

Halloween like this? Maybe even his life, if she didn't stem the bleeding fast.

Blue and red flashing lights painted the victim's ashen face as a police cruiser pulled up with a piercing "Whoop." A uniformed cop pushed through the crowd. "I've got this, ma'am. You need to back off."

"I'm a doctor," she snapped. "Where's that ambulance?"

"At least thirty minutes out. We only have one, and some idiot kids were horse playing around a beach bonfire."

The first of her runners arrived with clean towels and a water bottle. Saline would be better, but this would have to do for now. She twisted the bottle open, moistened the towel, and applied pressure, carefully keeping her voice calm. "You're gonna be okay, hon. We'll get you to the hospital and take good care of you."

Liv dropped to her knees beside Addy. "Vietnam vet, highly intoxicated. According to witnesses, he freaked out when these two chuckleheads crashed the VFW party."

"It was just a joke," the other victim moaned while the vampire bartender patched him up with gauze and tape. "We just wanted to scare the old guys. Ow, that alcohol fuckin' hurts."

"Serves you right, numbnuts," the vampire hissed.

"Liv, hold pressure here." Addy placed her friend's hands over the bloody towel.

While Liv murmured reassurance to the fallen man, Addy pulled the cop aside. "This guy is in danger of bleeding out while we wait for transport. We need to get him to the hospital *now*."

Chapter Sixteen

♥

Clutching his pirate hat over his pounding heart, Kieran watched the firefighters lift Addy's patient into their truck. Where the hell was the ambulance?

After subduing old Dave Budny, who melted into a puddle of tears once he realized his flashback freak-out had hurt two kids far more than their dumbassery deserved, Kieran had hovered as close as he dared to watch Addy work.

Simply awe-inspiring, the way she remained calm and commanding amid the chaos of panicked drunks. If she hadn't been there, that poor, stupid kid would've bled to death in the middle of Main Street.

Kieran had seen that boy and his buddies on the beach, whooping it up around their beer cooler and yelling ugliness at passing women. Probably never occurred to him that an old man with hair-trigger self-control would be his undoing.

While Halloween partygoers drifted back into the bar, Officer Jefferson handcuffed old Dave and lowered him into the police cruiser. Addy's friend approached Kieran, wiping her hands on her torn dress. "Well, that was a shitshow," she muttered. "Think anyone will step up for that poor man?"

"I'll swing by the VFW. I'm sure his vet buddies will look in on him."

"Does Trappers Cove have a support group for people like him?"

"Yeah. It's called happy hour at the VFW."

The woman scowled.

"Sorry, ma'am. I'm not making light of the problem. I'm sure you know how hard it can be to find mental health help these days, especially in a small town."

"I do indeed. Us military folks have it better than most civilians in that respect, and even on base, wait times for counseling can be way too long." She patted his arm. "By the way, Addy mentioned your oil rig fire. I hope you don't mind."

He shook his head. "I'm glad she has someone she can talk to about the important things."

"Do you have someone like that?" Her gaze held quiet compassion.

While he could call almost everyone in Trappers Cove a friendly acquaintance, outside of the therapy group he'd abandoned, Addy was the only person he felt comfortable opening up to. Hell, most of his neighbors didn't even know his proper name, a fact that hadn't bothered him until tonight.

He'd better remedy that self-imposed distance quick because if the perfect storm of triggers hit him like it had old Dave, who's to say he wouldn't spiral into madness, hurting himself or others?

Addy's friend gently gripped his arm. "Tell you what. Let me ride along to the VFW and make sure everyone's okay. Then we can talk about trauma therapy resources on our way to the hospital."

"All right, let's go."

"Like attracts like," his mother would say in her lucid moments, and his Addy—unselfish, duty-driven, compassionate—had drawn to her a friend with the same admirable qualities. Doctor Liv had a better chance than most at getting through to the walled-off vets who gathered in that dingy bar.

Over the past year or so, Kieran had inched toward acknowledging that he needed help, but tonight's events delivered a hard shove right to the gut. For Addy's sake, he'd do his damnedest to conquer his demons—before they destroyed his best chance at happiness.

Holding a surgical mask to her face, the night-duty medical assistant poked her head through the OR door. "MedEvac chopper's ten minutes out. And Chief Hawthorne would like to talk to Doctor Connor as soon as she's available."

"Thanks, Kit." PA Jorge Rosado handed Addy a pair of forceps.

"Our patient will be ready." Buzzing with satisfaction and relief, Addy finished the surgical repair that stabilized the young man for transport to the trauma center in Portland.

"Our Caden got lucky tonight," the nurse anesthetist remarked. "If you hadn't been on site, he wouldn't have made it."

"Not just me." Addy tied off the last suture. "All of you too."

The NA, who serviced three regional hospitals on the Washington coast, had been nearby chaperoning her son's high school Halloween dance, and the physician's assistant on duty had served in a modular field hospital in Iraq, so he was well qualified to double as a surgical nurse. Without their help, the young man on the table would definitely have bled out.

Later, in the scrub room, PA Rosado peeled off his bloody gloves. "Thank God I won't have to tell Caden's parents he died—and how."

Addy squeezed his shoulder. "The hardest part of the job, for sure. I'm glad you were here to help."

Her assistant chuckled. "Gotta say, even the worst cases here are easier on my soul than what we encountered in Fallujah."

"How'd you end up in Trappers Cove?" Addy asked.

"My gramps left me his house here. It's a nice town. Quiet. Good people." He tossed his surgical gown into the bin. "Like Caden's parents. Salt of the earth, but too permissive with their late-in-life miracle baby."

What would it be like, Addy wondered, to know her patients as well as Rosado did? With frequent changes of duty station, military life didn't lend itself to that kind of relationship. Another point against staying in the Army.

"Will you brief Caden's parents?" she asked. "They'd probably rather hear from a trusted friend than a stranger."

"Of course." He gave her a warm smile. "And don't you be a stranger, Doctor Connor. Come back and see us next time you're in town."

Addy grumbled to herself as she finished her post-op clean-up. What an outrage for a community hospital to have only a physician's assistant on duty on Halloween, of all nights! The on-call doc, a family practitioner, had taken his sweet time coming in to stitch up the other kid's shredded hand.

Trappers Cove hadn't had an on-call surgeon in years, according to the PA. Typical small-town hospital, chronically understaffed and unable to lure highly paid specialists.

Jittery on the tail end of the adrenalin rush that fueled tonight's work, Addy heaved a shaky sigh. Her patient had survived, but he had a long, rough recovery ahead of him. And for what? The momentary thrill of traumatizing an old man? This kind of senseless injury was the absolute worst.

And now came the inevitable paperwork.

Kieran was waiting on a bench opposite the nurse's station, still in full pirate regalia and idly flipping through a celebrity gossip magazine. As soon as he caught sight of her, he sprang to his feet and enveloped her in his arms.

God, it felt so good to be held by him, and in two more days, she'd have to leave him. She squeezed her eyes shut to hold back brimming tears.

"You're shaking, love. Here." He slid out of his velveteen coat and draped it around her shoulders.

"Aftereffect of an adrenalin surge," she assured him, but all the same, it was lovely to be wrapped up in his warmth and woodsy scent.

He pressed a soft kiss to her forehead. "You're a hero, Addy."

She snuggled into his embrace. "I just did what needed to be done."

And that's why she had to leave him for a while. She had other duties to attend to before she could consider her own desires.

Kieran went to fetch coffee and snacks from the vending machines while Police Chief Jess Hawthorne interviewed Addy and thanked her for saving the victim's life.

"Chief, what will happen to that poor old man?"

"Dave? I imagine the judge will go easy on him if he commits to treatment for his PTSD. Of course, that means leaving town, and he's gonna hate that. Dave keeps his orbit small: home, the Food Co-op, church, and the VFW."

Stepping up beside them, Liv tsked. "It's a damn shame help isn't available closer."

"True," the chief said, snapping her notebook shut. "Small-town life comes with trade-offs."

Liv gave Addy a pointed look. "Yeah, but health-care access shouldn't be one of them."

"What's that stare about?" Addy asked once the cop left. "You know I can't give that old man the kind of help he needs."

"No, but this town's badly in need of someone with your skills. And isn't this what you've been looking for? A quiet home where you can breathe, recover, sink some roots?"

Addy scowled and searched the room for Kieran, or anyone who could interrupt Liv's too-sharp questioning.

From down the hall came a metallic clang, a thump, and a string of Irish-inflected curses.

"When did I ever talk about sinking roots?"

Liv ticked off on her fingers. "Over coffee last week, at Johnson's retirement party, on our last girl's weekend."

That's the trouble with befriending someone with a mind like a steel trap—they build up an arsenal of your own words to use against you.

Kieran finally returned with three half-full paper cups and cellophane-wrapped Danish. "Sorry, ladies. Uncooperative machines."

Liv took her cup and moved off to chat with the nurses, and to give Addy and Kieran space, no doubt.

Kieran sat on a padded bench along the wall and pulled Addy down beside him. While she sipped her lousy coffee and let its warmth infuse her exhausted body, he massaged her tense neck muscles, which melted like butter under his firm touch.

"You were amazing tonight, Addy. You could do a lot of good here, you know."

She groaned with pleasure and a tinge of regret. "I wish it were that simple."

"I suppose your friend is staying at your place?"

"Afraid so." She leaned onto his shoulder.

"I like her." He nuzzled her hair. "Smart. Kind. We talked a lot tonight. She gave me a different perspective."

"Yeah?" She took a big bite of bland, sugary pastry.

"Tonight was the kick in the arse I needed." He swiveled to face her. "Addy, I'm going back to therapy. I can't let myself get like old Dave, haunted and brittle and ready to snap." He seized her icing-smeared hand and kissed her knuckles. "I want to be strong enough to deserve you."

Tears stung her eyes and spilled down her cheeks. "Kieran, it's not a question of deserving. You're a wonderful man, kind and wise and so sexy you make my knees weak." She stroked his jaw, his beard scratchy-soft under her palm. "I love you, my handsome pirate. You're helping me face my demons in a way even Liv couldn't."

"I am?" His smile glowed with joy and hope, so sweet and beautiful she had to kiss him in front of the ER staff, something she'd never have done before meeting this dear, brave man.

But saying 'I love you' was the easy part. Building a love strong enough to last? That would take time, courage, honesty...and she had a lot of baggage to unload before she could make herself fully available to him. He deserved her full attention, and right now, she couldn't give it.

"I've been stupidly prideful," she admitted, "thinking I could handle my PTSD on my own. Now I see how important it is to accept help—and not just from sympathetic friends." She smooched his lips again. "But I'll never heal until I close out some ugly unfinished business. Will you wait for me?"

"Until the tides still, Doc." He pulled her onto his lap. "Until the world stops spinning."

Giggling, she wound her arms around his neck. "It won't take that long, love. And I'll miss you every second I'm away." She rained kisses over his beaming face. "Think you can sleep tonight?"

"Without you? Probably not much."

"Hey Liv," she called, and her tactful friend turned to face them.

"Here." She tossed her keys. "Make yourself at home. I'm going to Kieran's tonight."

Liv grinned widely. "Don't you want to pack a bag first?"

"Nope." She kissed Kieran's forehead. "I've got all I need."

Chapter Seventeen

While Snoot snuffled nervously around her feet, Addy packed the last of her things into a shopping bag. Poor pup. He sensed change in the wind, and change made him nervous.

She gave his ears a scratch. "Me too, buddy."

After the Halloween brawl and subsequent surgery, Kieran had soothed her to sleep with gentle kisses and Irish-lilted declarations of love. Yesterday, after shooing the last tourists through the lighthouse doors, he'd rushed to her rental cottage for another night of lovemaking that started slow and sweet and ended hot and fierce, followed by cuddles, laughter, and talk until neither could keep their lids from falling.

But Saturdays were Kieran's busiest day at the lighthouse, so Addy had plenty of solo time to think, and stew, and cogitate. Slowly, one painful clunk at a time, the pieces of her new life were falling into place.

Colonel Okafor had taken the news well. "We'll miss you, Addy. You're a fine surgeon and an outstanding officer. But if it's time to go, well—you've earned a respite. I wish you all the best in your next chapter."

Just what form that next chapter would take depended on a job search that would last weeks, maybe months, and a mountain of paperwork she was dreading. Kieran said he'd wait, but the bureaucracy involved in job hunting would try the patience of a saint, and they were just two flawed, haunted mortals trying to help each other out of a dark place. It was going to be a long, hard climb.

Starting tonight.

While it was easy to fall in love with someone she was wildly attracted to, someone kind and funny and gorgeous, if they were going to create something lasting, they had to find enough common ground to build on.

After the past two nights in Kieran's arms, after soul-quaking sex and talking into the wee hours, her heart had no doubts. Her head, though? That stubborn organ needed more persuading.

In her journal, she'd prepared a list of questions to get them started, covering habits, preferences, priorities, hopes and dreams. If she was going to rebuild her life with Kieran at the center of it, she needed to know more about the man than how good he felt naked, his heavy, muscular body pressing hers into the mattress as he moved deep inside her...

She huffed a laugh. Yeah, keeping her mind on their shared future and out of Kieran's pants would require some serious discipline.

Drawn by her laughter, Snoot dropped into play posture, forequarters low, butt in the air, tail wagging a mile a minute.

"Okay, bud, let's take a beach break." She scratched the soft fur behind his ears. "I'll miss those almost as much as I'll miss Kieran."

"Closing time, folks. Good evening to ya." Kieran gave his last visitors—a talkative couple from Minnesota—a gentle nudge toward the door. If he couldn't dislodge these friendly barnacles, he'd be late for his date with Addy.

She'd asked to spend their last night together at his place, and he still had to shower, check the Irish stew bubbling in the slow cooker, and make sure the bed linens and bathroom were up to snuff.

This wasn't goodbye, he reminded himself, just a temporary parting while she sorted out that 'unfinished business' she spoke of. Over tea and bagels this morning, she'd promised him big news but refused to give him even the slightest hint. The suspense was killing him.

He was arranging a lopsided bouquet of supermarket daisies and sea grass when a soft knock and a loud woof announced their arrival.

"Right, here we go," he muttered, giving his breath a final check. He needed tonight to be perfect—cozy, sexy and memorable enough to lure her back ASAP.

As soon as he opened the door, Snoot nearly bowled him over, wiggling joyfully from snout to tail tip.

"Easy, now," Addy scolded through her laughter. "We want him in one piece."

"Welcome, love." Ever since that magic word left her lips two nights ago, he'd been repeating it, trying out its shape in his mouth, whispering it during his park ranger duties, singing it in the shower. A new buoyancy filled him, transforming his steps into a giddy dance, brightening the colors around him—and still, an element of fear nibbled the edges of his happiness.

She was leaving tomorrow, and he worried the magic they'd found might pop like a soap bubble if stretched over a long distance.

So that was his goal tonight: make a plan to stay in touch and get to know her better despite their separation.

He wrapped his arms around her and held her close, breathing in her fresh scent, relishing her softness, her warmth. He needed to memorize this moment, a comfort he'd need in the rough days ahead when Addy would only be a voice on the phone, a moving picture on his screen.

"Mmm, you feel so good," she murmured into the crook of his neck, and his cock stiffened at her hungry tone. He'd get her into bed soon enough, though. Before that, they had more important ground to cover.

When Addy finally let go, her beautiful features were etched with sadness. "Our last night."

"Just for now, love," he corrected her, hoping she couldn't hear the tightness in his voice.

"Of course." She slid her hand down his back and—heavens!—inside his trousers to squeeze a big handful of his arse. "No worries there, Keeper. I'm coming back to you. Now—" She wriggled her hips against his. "Food first, or a pre-dinner quickie?"

This time, Snoot didn't protest their long, deep, steamy kiss, instead making himself comfortable on the cushion Kieran had provided near the hearth.

But Addy's phone did protest—with a snatch of AC/DC.

"Highway to Hell?" He chuckled into her hair.

"Ugh." She dug the phone from her pocket, silenced it, and tucked it away again. "It's my Aunt Tish, chief flying monkey for my mom's cause."

"Flying what now?"

"You know, from *The Wizard of Oz?*"

He shrugged at the unfamiliar name.

"Wow." She slid her hands into his hip pockets and grinned up at him. "We're going to have so much fun learning each other's cultural references. But in the meantime..." She kissed him again, then drew his lower lip between her teeth and gave it a tiny nip that shot fire through his veins.

He gripped her hips and angled his, teasing her with shallow thrusts. "Well, I was planning to woo you over my gran's Irish stew, but—"

Her phone vibrated beneath his fingers.

"Ugh." She wriggled from his grasp and pulled the electronic pest from her pocket. "Is one night's peace too much to ask?"

"Sounds like it is." He smooched her cheek. "If you need to talk to your monkeys, I'll take Snoot out for a walk."

She hesitated, a scowl on her kiss-stung lips. "I hate to interrupt our evening, but it's high time I put this to rest." She hovered her finger over the screen, then raised an eyebrow. "You want a sample of what I'll be dealing with while we're apart?"

Her offer floored him. "You want me to listen in?"

"Why not? You're a wise person. Maybe you can give me perspective."

He pressed a kiss to her temple. "Then I'd be honored."

The phone stopped buzzing, then started again.

"Oh, crap. It's a video call." She angled the screen away from his face, rolled her shoulders like a boxer warming up, and pressed Accept.

At first, Kieran found the caller's tirade amusing, like a panel guest's rant on one of those trashy talk shows his ma had loved. But as the woman grew shriller, he found himself struggling not to snatch Addy's phone and give the venomous cow what for.

"Your mother's nerves are shot, Miss Addy," the woman insisted in her nails-on-a-chalkboard voice. "She needs your help, and it's about damn time you stepped up."

Addy's jaw muscles ticked. "What exactly is her diagnosis, Aunt T?"

"Diagnosis?" The woman's snort rang out loud and clear. "Excuse me, Doctor High Horse, for not knowing the medical terms. My sister is sick and old, and she can't handle living alone anymore, so someone's gotta take care of her."

A voice from Kieran's past wheedled into his memory.

You're abandoning us too? This is the thanks we get after devoting our lives to our children—a blatant lie, because his parents had done the bare minimum to stay out of trouble with the authorities.

And so it was with parents of their ilk, his and Addy's. In their view, it was kids' job to sacrifice for parents, not the other way around.

"You know what your problem is, Addison?" the auntie shrieked. "You're selfish. Always have been."

Growling low in his throat, Snoot stalked over to stand at Addy's feet. His hackles bristled.

Damn right, pup.

Anger sizzled along Kieran's nerves. How dare this shrew abuse the woman they loved? Before he could stop the impulse, his hand shot out and grabbed Addy's phone.

"Now it's your turn to listen, Tish." He spat the words out like shards of glass. "Addy is the least selfish person I know, and her work is damned important. She's saved more lives than there are people in your puny town. There's a nationwide shortage of doctors, and you expect her to sacrifice her career to take over her mother's care? Explain to me how that makes sense."

Snoot chimed in with a resounding woof.

"Who the hell are you?" the red-faced woman demanded.

"Someone who cares about Addy a helluva lot more than you do."

Addy pried the phone from his fingers and shot him a look that would have silenced a rabid wolf.

"I'm sorry," he whispered, flushed with shame for his loss of control, but still furious.

Unfazed, Aunt Tish continued her barrage. "All Betsy's other kids have their own families to worry about. Addy's the only one who's single."

Kieran put his arm around Addy and snugged her to his side. "No, she's not."

The woman glared. "A boyfriend is not the same as family, Addy. Blood matters more than some foreign—"

Before she could finish her insult, Kieran barked, "You really want to talk to a surgeon about blood? As if you had the tiniest notion in your pea brain about what Addy's been through, what she's sacrificed to help others."

"Kieran." Addy hit Mute and shot him a warning glance. The fire in her eyes appeased him—as long as it was directed at her asinine aunt and not at him.

But it was him, and not her phone, she was glaring at.

Crap on a cracker, I'm an eejit.

"Forgive me, Addy. I've overstepped by miles, but you can't let this woman bulldoze you."

"I've got this," she assured him, her chin firm, then restored the sound, catching her aunt mid-tirade.

"Enough, Tish," she snapped, her voice firm and commanding. "Here's what I'll do. Since no one in the family is willing to oversee Mom's care, I will fly out there and meet with her doctor. I will interview in-home caretakers. I will check out assisted-living facilities. And I will hire a lawyer to oversee Mom's financials and make sure her estate is set up according to her wishes."

She gave Kieran's waist a squeeze. "Here's what I will not do. I will not move back to Smithsville, and I will not listen to one more word about how my life doesn't measure up to your narrow ideas."

"Now listen here, Missy—" her aunt spluttered.

"Not one word, Tish."

And miracle of miracles, the woman shut her trap.

"I'll text Mom my arrival date. And my departure date." With a stab of her finger, she ended the call, then groaned and mashed her face into Kieran's chest.

He hugged her tight, alarmed to feel her shoulders shaking.

"Easy, love," he murmured into her hair. "It'll be fine. I'm so proud of you for standing up to that harpy."

When she raised her flushed face to his, he realized it was laughter making her tremble.

"I'm proud of me too." She grabbed the back of his neck and pulled him in for a long, sweet kiss. "God, I feel marvelous! Why did I wait so long to do that?"

"Dunno," he said against her lips. "Because you're a good person?"

She linked her hands behind his neck and leaned back to regard him with an amused grin. "I've let ideas about duty keep me from seeing my family for what they really are—self-serving bigots who resent me for escaping their control. They decided long ago I was the family's odd duck, and they're determined to net me back into the stagnant pond they're all swimming in." She giggled. "And now I'm picturing Aunt Tish quacking in outrage."

"That describes her voice perfectly." He slid his hands down her back to rest on the swell of her luscious ass. "It's not fair they're counting on you to do all the work for you mother."

"I know." She kissed the tip of his nose. "But I need to see for myself what's going on with her. Chances are fifty-fifty she's just cranky, but she might have real health problems."

He kissed her again. "You're a good daughter, Addy. Don't ever doubt that."

"Thank you. And I'm not doing it for them, you know. I'm living up to my own values. No matter what accusations they throw at me, I'll leave Smithsville knowing I've done my duty."

"And afterward?"

Holding his gaze, she sucked in a deep breath. "Right, my news. I've given the Army eleven years, more than fair repayment for medical school. I'm proud to have served my country, but I need to tend to my own wounds now. And Trappers Cove is the best place I can imagine to do that."

"Addy?" he croaked, hardly daring to believe his ears.

"My military commitment ends in December, and I'm officially job-hunting. I've set up an interview with Trappers Cove's hospital director."

Kieran's heart cartwheeled. Too overwhelmed to speak, he lifted her off her feet and spun her around with a whoop of pure joy. Snoot joined their dance, merrily galloping in a circle around them.

"Oh, crap." Addy wiggled free and crouched to hold her pup's face in both hands. "What am I gonna do with you while I'm in Nebraska?"

Kieran squatted beside her. "Addy, it would be my honor to keep him while you're away." He ruffled the dog's broad head, and the beast flopped over on his back for a belly rub.

"See? He likes me." He gave the pup a tickle that made him squirm and whimper with glee.

She joined him in a four-handed dog massage. "We both adore you, Kieran. I just show it in a different way. Though you do make me whimper."

She nudged him, and he toppled onto his arse, laughing and pulling her down with him. Snoot clambering on top of them, bathing both their faces in doggie kisses, which only made them laugh harder.

"Enough," Addy finally shouted. "Snoot, bed."

Head down, the dog slunk to his cushion by the fireplace.

"We love you, buddy," Addy assured him, "but Kieran and I need some private time. Isn't that right, Keeper?"

"Absolutely right." He grinned so hard his cheeks ached.

She smooched the tip of his nose, his forehead, the eyelids he closed on a sigh—then claimed his mouth in a deep, drugging kiss.

He tightened his grip on Addy and thanked whatever powers may be for saving him from a fiery death so he could meet this amazing woman, for opening her heart to a deeply damaged man, for bringing her to Trappers Cove.

When they finally came up for air, Kieran rose and pulled her to her feet. "Another hour in the slow cooker won't hurt tonight's dinner, you know."

"An hour?" She grabbed a handful of his arse and squeezed. "Maybe for the first round."

God, he loved this woman!

Chapter Eighteen

♥

Addy set her empty bowl on the nightstand and wiped her gravy-smeared lips. "That, my love, is the most delicious stew ever to be stewed in the history of stew."

Chuckling, Kieran plucked another tissue from the box and dabbed at the corner of her mouth. "Whatever it takes to keep you coming back for more."

"Well, naked dinner after mind-blowing sex is a pretty powerful incentive. Here, you've got a drop in your beard." She blotted gravy from his jawline, then kissed him for the hundredth time that night. "And you, Keeper, are the most delicious man ever to...um..."

Chuckling, he gripped her ass with both hands and pulled her atop him. "To what, love?"

She straddled him and sat up to drink in his beauty: warm hazel eyes glimmering with mischief, kiss-swollen lips, muscled chest and shoulders and arms that had become her refuge.

Her well-pleasured core throbbed at the sight of him laid out before her, and so did her well-loved heart.

Kieran's quiet, steady support had finally given her the push she needed to confront her family—though not so quiet tonight. She'd never forget the shock on Aunt Tish's face when

Kieran tore her a new one, his Irish brogue thickening with each sharp word.

The promise of their shared future would buoy her through the hard days to come, when she rode the wave of her long-overdue defiance right through Bumfuck, Nebraska.

Addy twirled her fingertip in the auburn hair dusting Kieran's pecs. "You are simply too glorious for words."

She pecked his lips, but he was having none of her chaste kisses. With a seductive snarl, he rolled her onto her back and pressed his pelvis between her splayed thighs.

Addy squirmed beneath him. "Scratchy crumbs on the sheets."

"Note to self," Kieran said with a chuckle, "Get one of those little crumb-sucker vacuums."

"Eventually, we'll have to give up this habit of post-sex snacks in bed."

"I suppose." He lowered his head and circled her nipple with his tongue. "But for now, if you're in my bed, I don't want to leave it." He sighed and rubbed his cheek between her breasts. "I'll miss you, Addy girl."

She stroked his soft curls and closed her eyes against the bittersweet pang washing through her. "Let's video call every night."

"And every morning." He started in on her other nipple, teasing it to a tingling peak.

Addy arched into his caress. "I've never tried phone sex before. Are you up for it?

His laughter tickled her skin. "I'm not a young man, Addy, but with you, I find myself up most of the time." He trailed kisses down her belly. "You know, I'm still hungry."

Gasping, Addy sank into the pillows as Kieran's magical tongue set her alight.

***

With Addy's name on his lips, Kieran tumbled over the edge into a thundering climax.

In all his lonely years of self-pleasure, he'd never come this hard. But the sight and sound of Addy crying out on his tablet screen amplified his bliss beyond anything he'd ever experienced—except, of course, for when she wrapped herself around him, her inner walls clutching him tight, her nails scraping his back.

Though almost eighteen hundred miles separated them—he'd looked it up—seeing her undulate in her hotel bed, eyes fluttering, teeth sunk into her plump lower lip, her chest and face flushed as she arched into her orgasm...Jaysus, the woman was simply magnificent.

When his breath settled enough for speech, he wiped his cum-striped belly and lay back on the pillows. "Thank you, love. I needed that."

"Me too." She swiped the dark hair off her forehead. "Especially today. God, I miss you."

A soft whuff sounded outside the bedroom.

"Someone wants to say hello."

Kieran pulled on his undershorts, because Addy's dog had a tendency to poke his cold nose into sensitive places, then opened the door. The Lab bounded onto the bed, tail whipping as he searched for the sound of his mistress's voice.

"Snoot!" Addy gushed, "How's my buddy?"

Perplexed, the pup snuffled through the sheets. Finding to trace of Addy's scent, he quickly lost interest and rolled onto his back for a belly rub.

"Give him extra pets for me," Addy said with a fond smile. "I miss him almost as much as I miss you."

Secretly, Kieran suspected it was more like fifty-fifty. Snoot was feckin' adorable and kept him laughing through their evenings together.

"Aye aye, Doc." He saluted with his free hand.

Addy's expression shifted—still smiling, but tinged with sorrow. "Speaking of military matters, my terminal leave was approved."

"So, you don't have to return to the base?"

"No." She snapped her fingers. "Just like that, I'm no longer employed by Madigan Army Medical Center. It feels—"

"You have regrets?" Kieran asked, his cheek propped on his bent arm.

She drew a deep breath. "No. It's a big change, but it's the right decision for me." Her lips compressed in a firm line. "About damn time I put my own needs first."

"Amen." Pride filled his chest. His Addy was a strong woman, whip-smart and determined. Once she set her course, nothing would hinder her.

Funny way to get to know someone, but the hours they'd spent video-chatting over the past two weeks—over his morning tea and her diner breakfast, between visitors to the lighthouse, on beach walks with Snoot, on his evening grocery run, and in his lonely bed—had deepened their connection considerably.

Not that Kieran's bed was completely lonely. Snoot had his own bed beneath the window, but Kieran usually woke in the night to find the dog curled against his side.

"Got a call from your friend Liv," he told Addy. "She put me in touch with a support group in Westport. Might even try some of those woo-woo therapies—tapping, lucid dreaming, whatever it takes."

Addy snuggled into her stack of pillows. "I'm proud of you, Kieran."

"Thank you, love. That means a lot. How's it going in Bumfuck?

She rolled her eyes. "Awful. Today my cousins and aunts ambushed me for an 'intervention,' hoping to cure me of my wanderlust." She snorted a laugh. "They've been watching too much Dr. Phil. And get this! Mom's doctor confirmed that, other than high blood pressure and a touch of sciatica, she's remarkably healthy and strong for her age. He's setting her up with a therapist to talk through her anger issues."

Her smile slid away, and she stroked her phone screen with her fingertip. "I miss you like hell, but it took coming out here to prove things really are as bad as I remembered. In fact, they're worse. My family lives in an alternate universe fueled by gossip, social media, and reality TV. When I come home next week, I'll leave with a clean conscience. I won't allow them to steal one atom more of my happiness."

He hugged a pillow to his chest, the way he yearned to hold Addy. "And what makes you happy, love?"

Her dreamy smile bloomed again. "You do. Trappers Cove does. Helping patients does. Using my skills. Breathing in the salty sea air and falling asleep to the sound of the surf. But mostly you."

She rolled onto her back and held her phone overhead, her hair flowing over the pillow like dark water. "Any sign of the ghost?"

"Mmm hmm." It had been a long day, and his lids were getting heavy. "Saw her last night, out on the bluff. I called to her, but she didn't turn around this time." It hurt his heart to see the White Widow, endlessly searching, endlessly lonely—especially now that he knew what she was missing.

Addy sighed and wound a lock around her finger. "Poor restless soul." She covered a yawn with the back of her hand.

Snoot echoed her yawn, head propped on Kieran's thigh.

"I'll be home soon, Buddy." Addy's musical laugh had become Kieran's favorite sound. "Just a few more days, and then you and Kieran and I are going to have the best beach walks. But now, it's time for sleep."

He reached for the End Call button. "Good night, Addy. I love you."

"I love you too, my handsome keeper."

Epilogue

❤

Snoot knew something was up, and it wasn't just the delicious smells wafting from the kitchen. Never having seen Addy decorate for the holidays, the poor pup was perplexed by all the sparkle and fuss.

Until this year, she'd been content with a tiny, pre-decorated tree from the base florist. But for the past two days, she and Kieran had filled every corner and surface with fresh Christmas greenery and kitschy ornaments they'd bought together in Trappers Cove. Her favorite was the green, glittery alien waving from his tinsel-trimmed UFO—from Souvenir Galaxy, of course.

Whining softly, Snoot snuffled his way from the kitchen, where Kieran was assembling a huge cheese platter, to the dining room, where Addy was arranging holly and red hypericum berries in her grandmother's milk glass vase. Satisfied with her centerpiece for their holiday gathering, she stooped to reassure the anxious Lab.

"Easy, Bud. It's just a party. You'll get lots of belly rubs, and probably a belly ache from all the snacks." She adjusted his red and green bow tie, cupped his furry face, and smooched the top of his head. "Because you're irresistible! Yes, you are!"

Snoot licked her cheek. You'd think a dog smart enough to undertake the search and rescue training he was currently acing would learn that people don't like slobbery kisses, but nope. Ah well, they'd have to warn their guests—most of whom had already met Snoot, anyway.

Once Addy's U-Haul truck was spotted heading toward the lighthouse last month, word spread quickly—the new doctor was shacking up with the keeper. So even though she'd insisted this was just a casual gathering, bookshop owner Daphne warned her to expect a flood of housewarming gifts.

"You know how fast gossip spreads in a small town," the bespectacled bookseller teased.

At first, Addy was anxious about similarities between her childhood hometown and Trappers Cove, but she needn't have worried. TC people might be a bit too deep in each other's pockets for her taste, but it came from a place of caring and acceptance. So far, she'd seen no trace of the narrow-minded spite she grew up with. And the flood of visitors whenever one of their own was hospitalized warmed her heart.

These folks knew the true meaning of family—it had little to do with blood and everything to do with love.

Kieran emerged from the kitchen wearing his new apron, a black canvas number printed with *'Tis Himself.*

"Stew's ready. Ten more minutes on your tarta long long." After a few mangled attempts to pronounce tarte à l'oignon, he'd given up. "It's delicious," he declared over her practice Alsatian onion pie last week, "and that's all I need to know."

"You're delicious," she'd parried, and the pastry had gone cold as their tickle-fight quickly turned steamy and drifted into his bedroom.

Their bedroom, now complete with some new touches—a framed photo of her grandmother's garden, a new wardrobe cabinet for Addy, the dragon tree plant that stubbornly survived despite Addy's neglect, and Snoot's cushion, of course.

Kieran encouraged her to put her own touches on the cottage, but after years of traveling light, she'd held onto only a few sentimental items, including her cookbook collection, now housed on a shelf he installed beside the kitchen window.

He'd made space for her in every room, and though the little house was cramped by modern standards, she wouldn't want to live anywhere else. Together, they were making a home.

And tonight, they were entertaining friends together for the first time: some former colleagues from Joint Base Lewis-Mc-Chord, along with almost everyone she'd met in Trappers Cove.

Addy slid her arm around Kieran's waist and surveyed their party set-up. "Think we have enough dishes?"

"I do." He smooched the top of her head. "And if we run out, there's a stash of paper plates under the sink."

"Do we have enough salad?" She scanned the kitchen counter.

He grasped her shoulders and spun her to face him. "Relax, love. We have enough food to feed an army." He pecked her lips. "No pun intended."

He stepped back, but Addy grabbed his apron and towed him in for a longer, more satisfying kiss.

"That's better." She grinned against his lips when she felt the hard ridge poking her belly. "Ready for another go already? Didn't get enough this morning?"

His rumbly laughter lit Addy up like a Christmas tree.

"With you near, I'm always ready. Hence the apron. Don't want to alarm the neighbors."

With a sharp bark, Snoot barreled toward the front door.

"Speak of the devil." Kieran took Addy's hand and laced their fingers together. "Let's welcome our guests."

"Merry Christmas!" Annie Scott, the vintage shop owner, threw her arms around Addy. The funny, snarky redhead had become Addy's favorite TC friend. Within a week of moving to Trappers Cove, Annie had introduced her to the town's movers and shakers, including her tech billionaire husband.

"You look amazing, as always." Addy stroked the faux fur collar of her friend's beaded mohair sweater.

Annie beamed. "Thanks, doll. Kieran, you've met my husband, Michael Garwood?"

"Of course." Kieran shook the man's hand. "Fine thing you're doing for our hospital. We're grateful."

"Don't mention it." Michael gave his flame-haired wife a fond smile. "It's good to know that, when the worst happens, help will be available, thanks to Doctor Addy."

"Thanks to our new surgical suite," Addy corrected him. Construction had already begun on the new facility, and plans were underway to expand staffing for the increased patient load from the surrounding area.

"We brought you a little something." Annie handed Kieran a cellophane-wrapped antique teapot. "For your morning cuppa."

"Why, that's..." Kieran blushed to the roots of his hair. "Thank you, Annie."

"Quit blocking the doorway, you two," a gruff voice grumbled.

"Can it, Mo," his companion snapped. "We're not in a hurry."

"Speak for yourself, woman. I'm freezing my butt off out here."

Mo and Nabila Abadi, owners of Ali Baba Kebabs, smothered first Addy, then Kieran, in a tandem hug. Mo thrust a package into Addy's hands. "From our kitchen to yours."

"Moroccan spices," Nabila added and sniffed the air. "What smells so good?"

Kieran's grin held a note of pride—as well it should. He'd been working all day on today's feast. "Lamb stew, Irish soda bread, apple and berry pies, and Addy's delicious onion thing I can't pronounce."

"That'll warm you up." Nabilla smacked Mo's chilly butt and made way for the next arrivals: Daphne Lee from the bookshop, who brought a cookbook; her brother Ryan and his girlfriend Lilo, who brought non-alcoholic ginger beer from their Salty Dog Brewery; baker Garrett Becker, who brought sourdough loaves and butter cookies; plus Xander Anagnos, owner of Souvenir Galaxy, and his girlfriend Hannah Leoni, editor of the *Trappers Cove Beacon*, who brought a jar of organic dog treats and a kerchief printed with UFOs for Snoot.

And this time, not one of them called Kieran "Fred."

Bringing up the rear, organic farmer Jesse del Toro and his fiancée, Gemma Moore, brought potted herbs.

"For your windowsill garden," Gemma said, rubbing Jesse's muscular shoulder. "It's good for the spirit to see green growing things in wintertime. Aunt Zora sends her apologies. She had a last-minute Tarot emergency, but she and Marquetta will be along soon."

After introducing her new neighbors and Kieran to friends from the base, Addy urged everyone to dig in. As more guests arrived, the party spilled into the parking lot, where Kieran had installed a party tent and propane heaters borrowed from the Salty Dog Saloon.

Seated beside her at a picnic table, Kieran beamed. "Isn't this grand, Doc?"

"It really is." She scooted closer and kissed his cheek. "Your friends are so welcoming."

He nudged her arm. "Our friends."

"Think the ghost will put in an appearance tonight?"

"The moon is full, so she might."

Just then, Zora and Marquetta pulled up and hopped out of the librarian's VW Bus. Her woolen cape flapping, Zora hustled toward them, brandishing a small package.

"Sorry we're late, darlings." She gave Addy, then Kieran, a two-cheek kiss. "Psychic crisis. You know how it is, Addy."

"I suppose I do. Come inside. I'll get you something to eat."

Zora dismissed the offer with a wave of her be-ringed hand. "Pish tosh, we can serve ourselves. But first, here's a talisman for your new home."

Addy unwrapped a palm-sized black crystal with delicate striations that glistened beneath the party lights.

"It's beautiful," Kieran remarked.

"Black Tourmaline," Zora told them. "A powerful stone for deflecting paranormal activity and negative energy."

"Since you guys live in a haunted house," Marquetta added.

Kieran held the stone to the light, turning it over and over in his fingers. Addy recognized his furrowed expression—he was pondering a weighty question.

"You know," he said at last, "I'm not sure I want to chase the White Widow away. After all, this was her home before it was ours, and she brought Addy and me together."

Beneath the table, Addy gave Kieran's leg a squeeze. She'd had similar thoughts about their resident ghost since moving in. Though shivers always chased over her skin when the pale specter appeared, the widow's presence held no threat, only the echo of heartache.

"That's a lovely way to look at it." Zora folded Kieran's fingers over the stone. "But it's not a ghost repellant. Put this stone anywhere you want to transform negative energies into positive."

"I've got just the place." Kieran chuckled. "Beside Addy's phone charger. Those knucklehead cousins of hers haven't given up yet."

"Amen." Giggling, Addy placed her phone on the table and set the crystal on top of it. "Begone, evil spirits!"

Surrounded by friends old and new, they spent the rest of the night laughing and chatting and eating too much pie. Everyone showered Snoot with affection and snuck him treats. When the last guest departed and the overstimulated, overstuffed pup collapsed in his bed, Kieran brewed a pot of tea and grabbed woolen blankets from the chest. "Shall we kiss under the moon?" he asked, waggling his eyebrows.

Addy smooched his cheek. "Yes, please. A quiet moment with you is my favorite nightcap."

Out back, they snuggled on the bench and cupped their mugs, watching their plumes of breath twine with the tea's steam.

Addy leaned onto Kieran's shoulder, her heart wrapped in his calm, steady affection and her body wrapped in cozy wool.

"Happy, love?" he asked.

"Very. Tonight was wonderful. I feel..." she trailed off, and he waited, silently patient.

"That's one of the many things I love about you, Keeper. You always give me time to figure it all out."

His low laugh rumbled against her cheek. "Questions worth asking don't come with swift, easy answers."

"Except for one: who I want to spend the rest of my life with." She set her mug on the bench and cupped his face in both hands. "Thank you, Kieran."

Eyes glimmering with moonlight, he smiled. "For?"

"For loving me."

"Ah." He pulled her legs across his lap. "Likewise, Addy."

He glided his lips over hers, tender, unhurried, savoring their connection. With a happy sigh, she opened to his velvet tongue—until a familiar tingle raised the hairs on her nape.

Addy gripped Kieran's arm and broke their kiss on a sharp inhalation. "She's here."

The White Widow floated just past the railing, her transparent skirts trailing in the wind, her spyglass raised toward the horizon.

"Mary," Addy whispered.

In a slow, fluid motion, the spirit lowered her telescope and turned toward them, her eyes bottomless, dark pools. For a long, silent moment, she hovered there, and Addy was filled with an eerie sense of connection to a woman long gone but still present.

Funny, she thought, how time flowed endlessly, out and back like the tides. Love lost and found, anchored to this beautiful place, once Mary's home, now theirs.

"Thank you," Addy murmured.

Like fog fading in the sunlight, the ghost evanesced, then vanished.

They never saw her again.

Thanks for reading! Read on for more books by Sadira Stone, including the rest of the ***Trappers Cove Romance Series*** and more! But first...

Reviews are the lifeblood of hard-working authors like me, so if you enjoyed Kieran and Addy's story, I'd be so thrilled and grateful if you'd leave a review—just a line or two explaining what you enjoyed about the book. Look for Write/Leave a Review on your favorite vendor's page or click on the stars; you'll usually find this info under the book's title. Thank you from the bottom of my heart!

And don't miss the rest of the ***Trappers Cove Romance*** series!

Passion in the Cards: An Opposites-Attract Metaphysical Beach Town Romance (novella)

Headstrong, homebody farmer clashes with freedom-loving hippie chick, but their blazing chemistry is unstoppable. Though Jesse knows bewitching fortuneteller Gemma will never settle down in their quirky beach town, he can't resist playing with fire. When a harmless secret backfires, Gemma discovers just how deeply she's wounded Jesse, and how desperately she wants to keep him.

Passionate Brew: An Enemies-to-Lovers Beach Town Brewery Romance (novella)

When a control-freak brewery owner is forced to partner with a prickly master brewer, their business and their hearts will never be the same. Working side by side ignites sizzling desire. But when a high-stakes craft beer competition arouses their fierce rivalry, can new love survive this battle of wills? Come to Trappers Cove for a sizzling enemies-to-lovers small town workplace romance.

The Billionaire's Christmas Castle: A Silver Fox Holiday Beach Town Romance (novel)

His billions can't buy what he craves most—her love. Can a spoiled tycoon and a fiercely independent entrepreneur cross an ocean of differences to forge a love that lasts past the holidays? Come to Trappers Cove for an Over-40 Christmas beach town billionaire romance that'll steam up your windows and warm your heart!

Love, Legacy, and Little Green Aliens: An Over-40 Beach Town Romantic Comedy (novel)

HEA vs. a curse, a ghost, and a plague of ETs. Inheriting his uncle's beach town souvenir shop is Xander's chance to prove he's escaped the family curse. But to transform the alien-themed embarrassment into an upscale galleria, he'll have to fight off Hannah, the gorgeous small-town journalist hell-bent on protecting Souvenir Planet. Caught in a battle of wills and sizzling desire, they discover the bizarre depths of Uncle Gus's alien obsession. Come to Trappers Cove for a steamy rivals-to-lovers rom-com full of found family, beachy fun, aliens, ghosts, and out-of-this-world mystery.

Sweet Summer Surprise: A Steamy Age Gap Beach Town Romance

She came to the beach to find herself—and found him. Forced to spend her annual beach vacation alone, divorcée Danielle Peters finds new confidence in the arms of a younger man. Matteo has only two weeks to convince her that, despite their age difference, their sizzling connection is so much more than a vacation fling. Come to Trappers Cove for a sweet, steamy, older woman/younger man summer romance with a fresh start that'll warm your heart.

Also by Sadira Stone

shy, strait-laced coworker at Bangers Tavern. But his sweet smile and quiet charm disarm her defenses just when she needs them most. When his grandma walks in on a steamy moment, fake-dating chaos ensues! Come to Bangers Tavern for spicy, opposites-attract, fake dating, BBW rom-com fun that ignites in all the worst ways—and the best!

Delicious Heat

Bangers Tavern chef Diego meets a woman who makes his heart sing. Trouble is, she's pregnant with another man's child. With one belligerent ex and two overprotective families intent on breaking them up, Anna and Diego need more than red-hot passion to pull them through. His career and her baby's future are on the line. Come back to Bangers Tavern for a spicy tale of forbidden love that will warm your heart...and other parts...and make you hungry for empanadas!

Sweet Slow Sizzle

Bangers Tavern's hunky bouncer Jojo has been crushing on server Lana for years, but her sole focus is keeping her orphaned brothers together in the only home they've ever known. When the boys' teen shenanigans land them in trouble, Jojo may be the only person who can save them. This slow burn, sizzling hot friends-to-lovers workplace romance celebrates the glorious chaos of 21st century family—the ones we're born into, and the ones we gather to our hearts.

Cupid's Silver Spark: A Bangers Tavern Novella

At Bangers Tavern's Anti-Valentine's Bash, Carla collides with a swoonworthy silver fox. Could a no-strings fling be the remedy for her tattered heart? He seems perfect for the job: suave, attentive, and oh so tempting. Trouble is, his real estate firm has the hots for her building. To keep her business, Carla must dare to trust the enemy. Will her silver fox prove a predator, or will Cupid's arrow strike true?

***Book Nirvana* Romance Series**

Welcome to Book Nirvana, an indie bookstore in Eugene, Oregon, where you'll find every flavor of bookish delight, a quirky staff who are as close as family, Lulu the all-wise shop cat, Coffee Dreams next door, and a dazzling collection of naughty books kept behind the red door in back. If you ask shop owner Clara nicely, she just might let you peek inside!

Through the Red Door

Two good men vie to heal a widow's heart—but it only holds room for one. Unless Clara Martelli finds a lifeline, her bookstore will close its doors forever. Her best shot at saving Book Nirvana is her late husband's collection of rare, racy books, but she's not ready to open that red door. And she's not ready to open her heart again, even if the two new men in her life tempt her to try. Come to Book Nirvana for chosen family, laughter and tears, sizzling passion, and a love triangle for the ages.

Runaway Love Story

Wrong time, wrong place, perfect guy. Aspiring art gallerist Laurel is stranded in Eugene, Oregon, where she must rescue the beloved auntie who rescued her. Running into Coach Dalton ignites a sweet flirtation that quickly turns spicy. They're both enduring the heartbreak of losing a loved one to dementia. But he wants lasting love, and she's only passing through.

Come to Book Nirvana for a steamy, funny, heart-wrenching tale of true love and second chances.

Love, Art, and Other Obstacles

On the cusp of launching her graphic arts career, Margot is all about freedom—no fences, no limits, and no more bigoted family. Between college, work at Book Nirvana, and a high-stakes art competition, she barely has time for her part-time girlfriend, much less a flirtation with her competitor, even if the cocky, ginger-bearded ceramics artist makes her question her "no strings" rule. Come to Book Nirvana for a red-hot love triangle that forces two young artists to redefine success, family, and freedom.

Please visit sadirastone.com and **subscribe to Sadira's bi-monthly newsletter** for bookish news, reader exclusives, and romance freebies.

About the author

Award-winning contemporary romance author Sadira Stone spins steamy, smoochy tales set in the U.S. Pacific Northwest. Her stories highlight found family, friendship, and the sizzling chemistry that pulls unlikely partners together. When she emerges from her writing cave in Las Vegas, Nevada (which she seldom does), she can be found shaking her hips in dance class, blowing bubbles with her granddaughter, playing her guitar (not very well, but improving!), exploring the Western U.S. with her charming husband, cooking up a storm, and gobbling all the romance books. For a guaranteed HEA and no cliffhangers ever, visit Sadira at sadirastone.com.

Visit Sadira on All the Socials!
https://linktr.ee/SadiraStone